PUZZLED

P.J. Nichols

ISBN 978-1980661689

Cover design by Thomas Paehler

For my son, Justin,
You are so awesome.

CHAPTER 1

While fiddling with a couple of twenty-sided dice in his left hand, Peter took another glance at the clock above the blackboard. It now read 1:36, only three minutes later than the last time he had checked. As always, Peter was incredibly bored by Mr. Pendleton's grade seven geography class.

"Isn't it amazing?" Mr. Pendleton said. "Doesn't the complexity of nature just fascinate you beyond belief?"

Peter's teacher seemed obsessed with taking simple and easy concepts, and stretching out the explanations as long as humanly possible. Today, he was trying to illustrate the difference between a tsunami and a tidal wave. And in an attempt to make it easier to understand, he had drawn dreadfully awful sketches for his audience of uninterested twelve-year-old boys and girls.

"So as you can clearly see," Mr. Pendleton continued, "these are two completely different

1

things. You would be shocked to know how many people, even grown-ups, confuse the two."

Peter looked up at the clock again. Somehow, it had only managed to move ahead by another four minutes. That meant he still had twenty minutes here, followed by an hour of an even more boring math class.

Peter was by far the cleverest student in the class. He was actually the top grade seven student in the school, and most likely had one of the highest IQs in the entire town. His mind worked like a super computer, easily understanding even the most complex things. When he was nine or ten years old, he had tried over and over to help others see how easy it was to learn. But he had given up on that by the time he turned twelve.

Since school provided nothing interesting or challenging for him, he kept his mind busy by playing complex games and solving puzzles and riddles at home.

To try to distract himself from the clock, he started looking around the room at the other twenty-three students. In particular, he focused on the girl sitting two rows in front of him. Nicola had been attending the same schools as Peter since they were in kindergarten, but she sure had changed in the last few months. She was much taller and thinner now, and exactly eighty-seven days ago, had shown up at school with braces.

Peter and Nicola used to play together when they were in elementary school, back when no one cared about whether their friends were boys or girls. They even walked together to junior high for the first few months. But a new school meant new friends, and Nicola's new group decided that Peter was too *weird and geeky*, and that she was better off staying away from him.

His daydreaming was brought to an abrupt stop by Mr. Pendleton. "Peter, could you please rejoin us all on planet Earth for a minute?" his teacher said. "We would be very gracious to hear, in your own words, what causes a tsunami. Not a tidal wave, a tsunami."

Peter was fairly embarrassed that Nicola was now looking his way, so he got ready to give a *textbook answer* to the question, one that would cause no giggles or glares. But just as he was about to speak, his elbow accidentally bumped the dice off his desk.

"C'mon Peter," Mr. Pendleton said. "You know you're not supposed to bring toys to class."

This caused at least half of the class to start laughing, the exact thing Peter had been hoping to avoid.

Red-faced, he bent down to pick them up. But just before his hand got there, the kid sitting in the desk beside him decided to kick them away. "You heard him!" the kid said. "No toys!"

They rolled a couple of meters and stopped directly under Nicola's seat. She picked them up right away, but wasn't sure if she should return them to Peter or give them to Mr. Pendleton.

"Nik, what are you doing?" one of her ditsy new friends asked loudly. "I wouldn't touch those if I were you. You don't know where they've been!"

Nicola spun around to look at Peter, but he was already staring down at his lap. She'd known him for a very long time, and didn't like seeing him suffer like this.

Mr. Pendleton walked down her row and took the dice from her hand. "Thank you, Nicola," he said. "Peter, you may collect these after school today. And don't worry, I won't play with them or break them or anything like that."

The class had a good laugh over that one too. Peter could feel his face getting even redder than before. He had a very pale complexion to begin with, and it quickly changed color whenever he got even slightly anxious. His current level of embarrassment was enough to make it almost purple.

With the dice ordeal finally over, Mr. Pendleton got ready to continue his lecture. But for some reason, he couldn't recall where he had left off. "Now where were we?" he asked himself aloud. "Hold on a minute, everyone. I need to check my notes."

Mr. Pendleton started filing through the mess of papers on his desk. And while he searched, students here and there began chatting quietly with each other.

Then the bell rang, and everyone packed up and headed out of the room. All twenty-four of them were going upstairs to math class next.

Peter joined the procession. What surprised him was that Nicola grabbed the dice off the teacher's desk on her way out. Of course, she did it in a way that none of her new friends noticed.

CHAPTER 2

Peter walked through the door of his math classroom just as the bell was ringing. Although he loved numbers, formulas, and calculations dearly, he really hated Mrs. Baird's class. She had quickly noticed Peter's math skills during the first week of school, and now used him as her *go to* student whenever she wanted to hear the correct answer. And on top of that, she had moved him to the front row, right in front of her desk. That way she could ask him to help grade quizzes and things anytime he finished his work early.

As he took his seat, he noticed the dice were in his desk. Nicola must have found a way to put them in there when no one was looking.

"Hey geek!" he heard from one of the jocks in the back row.

Peter was no stranger to being teased, especially by the guys on the football and basketball teams. But since they were so much

6

bigger than him, he did whatever he could to avoid any type of confrontation. As he had done so many times before, he ignored their name-calling again today.

"Can't hear us, geek?" another one said, much louder this time. "Oh, I guess you think you're too smart to talk to us, right?"

Thankfully, Mrs. Baird walked into the room, so the jocks immediately stopped teasing Peter. They didn't want to risk getting detention after school today, as that would mean they would miss their beloved sports practice.

Today's math class was so slow and boring that Peter felt himself nodding off a few times. Mrs. Baird's monotone voice seemed to magically lull kids to sleep.

When there was about thirty minutes left in class, his teacher walked towards the door. "I need to make a few photocopies," she said. "While I'm gone, please continue working on pages 118 and 119, QUIETLY."

Within seconds of her departure, Peter felt the familiar sting of being hit by a spitball. He wasn't sure why they were called spitballs, as they were actually just tiny pieces of crushed up paper. These little paper balls were wetted with spit, put in the end of a drinking straw, and shot out like bullets by blowing through the straw.

But Peter wasn't going to give whoever fired

the spitball the satisfaction of a reaction, so he pretended nothing had happened.

"Next one's going to be extra wet, loser!" one of the boys yelled. "And this time I'm aiming for your ear!"

Peter pulled his collar up as far as possible, hoping it would reduce the chance of the next one hitting his bare skin.

"Grow up, guys!" one of the other kids yelled in Peter's defense.

Peter recognized Neil's voice immediately. Neil was the scatterbrained kid, who also had very few friends at school. Like Peter, Neil was the victim of regular teasing, so he was just trying to stick up for one of his own.

"You want one instead?" one of the boys asked Neil. "I'd be happy to help!"

"If you do, you'll regret it!" Neil yelled back, standing up at his desk.

"Wow!" the leader of the jocks said to his buddies. "Aren't you so big and tough! Oh, we're soooooo scared!"

Before it escalated any further, the door opened and Mrs. Baird walked back in. The spitball culprits managed to hide their straws in time, but Neil was caught standing up. Mrs. Baird instantly assumed that Neil had been causing some type of problem.

"Neil Bannister!" she said loudly. "You clearly

were NOT paying attention when I told you to work quietly. So you have just earned yourself detention with me after school today. That's lucky for me, as I have tons of paperwork that I need help sorting."

Neil sat down without saying a word. Mrs. Baird was famous for doubling detention time for anyone who tried to argue with her.

"Show's over. Back to work, everyone," she said. "Unless any of you would like to join Neil after school?"

Everyone, jocks included, quickly picked up their pencils again. Mrs. Baird then began to "monitor" everyone's effort, which meant she walked slowly up and down the rows with her arms crossed.

But the monotony was broken up by a loud clap of thunder outside.

"Oh, not again," Mrs. Baird said, with a concerned expression on her face. "What on earth is with this crazy weather?"

Everyone looked out the window and watched the strange weather phenomenon. It was something which seemed to be occurring more and more regularly during the past few months.

"Maybe they'll cancel school again. Maybe we can go home early," Nicola said to a friend sitting close by.

In the span of only fifteen seconds, the clear sky

became as dark as night. Then a powerful wind started howling, and rain hammered down.

These sudden and extreme storms only lasted about five minutes, but were causing irreparable damage to buildings, homes, crops, and shops. And weather experts couldn't explain what was causing them.

The lights suddenly went out. It looked like the storm had knocked out the power again. Peter smiled. They were probably going to be sent home early today.

A few minutes later, the rain let up, the wind subsided, and the blue sky opened up. The school principal then came into each class quickly and announced that school was cancelled for the rest of the day. Everyone was to pack up and head home quickly and safely.

Cheers of joy could be heard around the room. Peter even noticed Mrs. Baird smile after hearing the announcement.

Peter jammed everything into his backpack and darted for the door. He was planning to stand just outside the classroom door, and thank Nicola about the dice on her way out. But Peter was accidentally blocked by Neil. Neil was on his hands and knees picking up papers which had fallen on the floor when he had tried to pack up too quickly. Peter gave up on his race for the door, and helped Neil pick up a few handfuls of loose notes.

"Here you go," Peter said to him. "And thanks for standing up for me."

"No biggie," Neil replied. "I hate those guys too." Once Neil had managed to stuff everything back in his bag, he bolted for the door. "And this storm just got me out of detention!"

As Peter walked out of the front doors of the school, he surveyed the mess. These sudden storms always left puddles and mud on most of the roads. It was going to make today's trek home slow and messy.

"It's muddier than it looks!" the principal shouted as students exited the school.

Peter had used his older brother Bradley's snazzy new mountain bike today. But he had taken it without asking, so he made a mental note to himself that he would need to give it a good cleaning when he got home.

He slowly and cautiously walked through the sloppy mess towards the bike rack. But when he got there, it was obvious that a huge amount of mud had gotten into the chain. There was no possibility of riding it home.

"You've got to be kidding me!" Peter said to himself. He was not looking forward to pushing Bradley's bike through the muck for the entire 1.56 km trip home.

CHAPTER 3

After ten minutes of mumbling and complaining to himself, he was finally getting close to the intersection he had to cross to get to Beaverbrook Street. Peter looked up as he approached the crosswalk, to double-check that there were no cars coming.

There weren't any cars in sight, but something else caught his eye. There was a very old man standing on the side of the road just before the intersection. Peter knew he had never seen this old guy before, and couldn't fathom how someone could end up lost in the middle of the day. Despite the fact that Peter just wanted to walk right past him, he remembered all of the lessons his parents had taught him about helping those in need. He felt more or less obligated to offer some assistance.

"I suppose I'm going to have to help this old weirdo," Peter muttered under his breath, making sure he said it quietly enough that the old man couldn't hear him.

The man appeared to be holding some sort of paper or map in his hand. That likely meant it was just a simple case of needing directions. The man had also noticed Peter approaching, and was clearly getting ready to ask something.

Peter decided to initiate the conversation. "Sir, are you lost?" he asked. "Maybe I can help."

After a brief pause, the old man replied, "Well, I do suppose I'm lost. But whether or not you can help is really a different question altogether."

Peter was a little surprised by this answer. "Try me," he said to the old man. "I've been living around here my entire life."

The man pushed the paper, which was a map, quite close to Peter's face. "I'm trying to get to the library. Central Library, on Leeds Street," he said.

Without even glancing at the map, Peter quickly answered, "Oh, it's easy to get there. Just keep going down this road until you—"

But the old man interrupted Peter with a loud, gross grunt. It was like he was preparing to spit or cough or something. Then he pointed at his right leg, which was thinner and shorter than the left one.

"I know *how* to get there," the old man said, "but there's no way my legs are going to walk me that far. If I have to walk more than half a kilometer, I'll collapse on the spot!"

The old man took a couple of very awkward steps to demonstrate his point. And as Peter watched him limp, his mind began doing what it did best, calculate.

Thirty seconds later, Peter offered up a newer and better suggestion.

"OK, then how about this?" Peter said. "Seventy meters down the road, you'll see the entrance to Mr. Wilden's farmhouse. Mr. Wilden is about eighty or so now, and he gets picked up every afternoon at around three by Mr. Wright, his neighbor, to go for coffee. They always head to the little coffee shop on Kade Boulevard, which is less than two hundred meters from the door of the library. And I'm sure they would let you ride in with them if you ask."

The old man listened intently. He nodded his head while listening, and a grin began to appear across his face.

"That's a fantastic idea," the old man said. "And you thought it up so quickly. You're a clever boy."

The old man began slowly limping down the road towards the Wilden house. Peter could no longer see his face, which meant he couldn't see he was grinning from ear to ear.

CHAPTER 4

About fifteen minutes after his encounter with the old man, Peter finally made it back home. His house looked like it had escaped today's storm relatively unscathed.

Peter's family lived in one of the larger homes in an area of town where everything had been built over twenty years ago. It was a sturdy and practical two-story house, with really ugly off-white stucco on the exterior walls. When Peter was five or six, he was regularly scolded for picking off the stucco. There were a few patches on the wall that he had picked almost bare.

Without checking to see if anyone else was home, he pushed Bradley's bike through the gate and into the backyard. Peter knew how angry his older brother would get if he found out Peter had borrowed his new bike without asking. He turned on the water for the outdoor garden hose, grabbed an old rag from the garage, and started scrubbing away at the mud. Peter was the *meticulous* brother, and Bradley was the *anything goes* brother. A quick cleaning would be enough to fool Bradley.

To help distract himself from this incredibly boring task, Peter decided to count how many seconds he had been doing it for. Even before his second birthday, Peter had fallen in love with numbers. He would count anything and everything he could.

His count was now up to 846, which he knew was exactly fourteen minutes and six seconds. Peter had always wondered why his mind had to be computing or calculating something.

He finished cleaning the bike and started pushing it into the garage. Just before he got there, he saw his younger sister skipping and whistling happily towards him. Sophia, or *Princess Sophie*, as she liked to be called, was quickly approaching her ninth birthday. Despite being fairly irritating and unbelievably ditsy, she always happily tried Peter's puzzles and games. Most of the time, she couldn't even understand the rules of the games. And she never even came close to solving any of the puzzles. But no matter how hard or confusing it was, she never gave up or complained.

"Brad's going to kill you when he finds out you used his bike!" she said to him in her high-pitched voice.

Playing it safe, Peter decided to get Sophia on his side. "He'll never know," he said, "if you don't tell him. And if you promise not to tell him, I'll take you to the mall on Saturday morning."

He figured this proposal had close to a hundred percent probability of being accepted. Sophia would never turn down the chance to go to the mall.

"Really?" she squealed in excitement. "OK, I promise! But if you don't take me first thing on Saturday morning, then I *will* tell him, and he'll beat the crap out of you!"

Peter realized that borrowing Bradley's bike today had been a mistake. He would stick to using his own from now on. He knew two hours at the mall with his bratty sister was going to be a bore, but it was the only way to avoid Bradley's angry wrath. Peter knew Bradley wouldn't hurt him by using kicks or punches. Bradley would do something much, much worse. He would break one of Peter's puzzles or games. And those were by far his most prized possessions.

CHAPTER 5

At precisely 7:37 the next morning, Peter walked out the front door to head to school. If he rode, he would be able to delay his departure until 7:52. But since he wasn't sure if the roads were still muddy or not, he chose to walk.

Just like every other morning, Peter began counting the number of steps it took to reach the end of the street. He knew it would take him an extra three or four steps today, as he had to walk around a small puddle of water at the end of the driveway.

He got to the corner on step 153. He knew he'd be taking another nine hundred or so more before reaching the intersection. After about eight minutes of walking, he noticed someone standing at the intersection again today. As he got closer, he quickly realized it was the same person as yesterday. And not only that, but the man looked as if he were waiting for Peter's arrival.

"Now this is a getting creepy," Peter said to himself as he got closer and closer to the old man.

Wanting to steer clear of any danger, Peter stopped walking when he was about two meters away from him.

With a tinge of sarcasm in his voice, Peter asked, "Lost again, sir? This is a pretty small town. It's tough to get lost in the same spot twice."

It appeared as if Peter's words had gone in one ear and out the other, as the man's expression didn't change one bit.

After a fairly long pause, the old man replied, "Lost? No. In need of your assistance again? Yes."

"My assistance?" Peter said hesitantly. "What do you mean?"

Peter took a few more steps back. He wanted to ensure that he was well out of the old man's reach.

"Don't run away!" the old man begged. "The reason I need your help is... well... I need some puzzles solved."

"Puzzles?" Peter said, having trouble hiding his interest. "What do you mean? And why me? You could ask anyone."

"Because you," the old man said, "are very clever. Remember the question I asked you yesterday? You were about the two hundredth person that I asked that exact same question to over the last six months. And none of the previous people were able to help.

Peter backed up even further. Now this old guy was making him feel really, really uncomfortable.

"Wait! Please wait!" the man begged, even more desperately than before.

Peter looked the old man directly in the eyes. "Just tell me what you want. And why," Peter said. "I have to get to school. I'm going to be late."

"As I just said," the old man explained, "I want you to help me solve some puzzles. Why? Well, I can explain all the details in due time. For now, I'll leave you with this."

The old man put a small cardboard box on the ground.

"Young man," he said, "you are very smart. But I only need your help if you are *exceptionally* smart. Try to solve this puzzle. If you can't solve it, then you'll never see me again. But if you can solve it, then I will *need* to see you again."

Then the old man turned around and slowly started to limp away.

Peter looked down at the box. He nudged it a few times with his foot. Once he had convinced himself that it wasn't some type of explosive, he made the decision to look inside.

"I hope there isn't something like a dead frog in here," he said jokingly to himself.

He used his foot to open up one of the flaps on the box. And its contents intrigued him significantly.

CHAPTER 6

Peter squatted down so he could get a closer look at what was inside. The box contained only three things. There was a carrot, a blue felt-tip marking pen, and small piece of paper with something written on it. He removed the paper from the box and stood up. The message was even more bizarre than the contents of the box.

> *Your tools: This box, a carrot, a blue felt marking pen*
> *Your task: Make a rabbit change color.*
> *(But you CAN NOT color the rabbit with the pen!!)*

"This just keeps getting weirder and weirder," Peter said to himself.

He read the note again, thinking about how absurd the whole situation was. He had just been asked by an old guy, who came out of nowhere, to make a rabbit change color! But Peter couldn't refuse a puzzle, regardless of whom or where it came from. He immediately started considering various possibilities of how to approach this one.

"I suppose," he said to himself, "I could use the felt pen to color the inside of the box, and then drop it on a rabbit. Then while it jumps and flips around inside, the ink will get all over it. That would make it change color."

Peter smiled smugly about his brilliant plan. But a few seconds later, he dismissed it.

"No, no, no," he said to himself. "That won't work. The ink would dry on the box before I'd have a chance to drop it on a rabbit."

Beads of sweat started to form on Peter's forehead, and his hands became clammy. His hands always got cold and wet like this when he was concentrating. Peter paced around the box, holding the pen in one hand and the carrot in the other. He mumbled to himself as he considered other possibilities. Then he stopped suddenly and raised both arms in the air, like a marathon runner who had just crossed the finish line.

"Ladies and gentlemen, I believe we have a winner!" Peter blurted out. "And it didn't even take me three minutes."

Beaming with pride, he put the carrot and felt pen back into the box and picked it up. He started jogging towards Mr. Wilden's farm, just down the road. He quickly ran up the front steps and rang the doorbell twice.

"Mr. Wilden!" Peter shouted, well before Mr. Wilden had even come to the door. "Mind if I play with your rabbits for a bit?"

"Who goes there?" asked Mr. Wilden. His hearing aids were not turned on, so he hadn't heard what Peter had said.

"It's Peter!" Peter said loudly, as Mr. Wilden slowly approached the front door. "Can I play with your rabbits for a while?"

"My rabbits?" Mr. Wilden said, looking a little confused. "Aren't you too old to be playing with rabbits?"

Peter thought up a suitable response quickly. "It's for a school science project," he said. "And it won't take long."

Mr. Wilden seemed convinced enough by this explanation. "For school, eh?" he said. "Sure. Knock yourself out!" Then Mr. Wilden turned around to walk back to his sofa.

Peter was moving as fast as he could now. He was excited to put his brilliant plan into action.

"Over there looks good," he said to himself, eyeing a muddy spot beside the shed.

He placed the carrot on the ground. Then he turned the box upside down, and gently placed it over the carrot. He took the pen, lifted up one end of the box, and carefully propped up that end with the pen. He had just created a beautifully simple rabbit trap.

"And that," Peter proudly announced, "is what you do to catch yourself a rabbit!"

Peter knew Mr. Wilden had at least thirty rabbits in or around his barn. That was the reason he had chosen to come here in the first place. He picked a light-colored one and carried it over to his trap. He placed it down gently, and then just like he had predicted, the rabbit quickly went for the carrot. It bumped the felt pen on the way in, causing the box to fall and trap it inside.

Peter then put his foot on top of the box, making it impossible for the rabbit to escape. He crouched down and put both hands on top of the box, and then lightly slid it back and forth a few times. He did this gently to ensure that the rabbit inside wouldn't be hurt by his little stunt.

After about thirty seconds, he lifted up the box. The mud-covered rabbit hopped away, with the end of the carrot hanging out of its mouth.

"Viola!" Peter shouted, impressed by his handiwork. "That was a piece of cake!"

Peter sat down on a log in front of the shed, and kept watching until the rabbit had gone behind a small bush. "That was too easy," Peter said aloud. "Too bad that old guy didn't have something harder."

"Be careful what you wish for," said a voice from

behind him.

Peter spun around quickly. The old man was less than two meters away, smiling and rubbing his hands together.

"Hey, wait a second," Peter said to the old man. "I know you didn't follow me here. I would have seen you behind me."

"So?" the old man replied, putting his hands in his pockets and shrugging his shoulders.

"So... that means... you got here before me," Peter answered. "But how did you know I'd come here?"

"Because," the man answered, taking a few steps closer to Peter, "I am also extremely good at solving things. I knew you'd come here because that's exactly what I would have done."

"OK, OK," Peter said, standing up so he could be at eye level with the old man. "But why do you care? Who are you? Are you a salesman from a toy store or magic store or something?"

The old man let out a giggle, which turned into a roaring laugh. Then his laugh became hoarse, and ended in a disgusting cough. Peter was worried for a second that the old guy was going to have a heart attack right then and there.

Once the old man had caught his breath enough to speak, he sat down. "I most certainly am not a salesman," he said, still straining a bit to breathe properly. "This is not about money, Peter. It's actually an extremely serious matter th—"

"Peter?" Peter said, rudely interrupting the old man mid-sentence. "How do you know my name?"

The old man was unfazed by the interruption. "I heard you say it when you were calling for Mr. Wilden," he replied. "Peter, give me fifteen minutes of your time, after school today. That's all I ask. Just hear me out. I'll be waiting for you by the big sign on the side of the highway. You know, the *Welcome to Clearville* sign. You certainly don't realize it right now, but your help is needed by more than just me. It's needed by everyone."

CHAPTER 7

Peter ended up arriving at school more than an hour late, but managed to give the principal a very believable excuse. He made up a little tale about what had happened while walking his sister to elementary school. He told the principal that his sister had tripped and scraped her knee badly, so they needed to go to a nearby home to ask for help.

All day at school, Peter found himself pondering the meaning of the old man's comment. Although he was confident in his ability to solve puzzles, he had no clue at all how his skill could be *needed to help everyone.*

"And your homework," Mrs. Baird said, "is to finish all of the review questions on pages 121 through 124."

The bell rang and Peter robotically started packing his bag. But he shot back to attention very quickly when he heard Nicola's voice. She was standing right in front of him, and looking directly at him.

"Hey, Pete," she said. "You've always been a whiz at math, right? Do you think you could, um, give me a hand with this homework? I mean, um, if you're not busy..."

Before she had a chance to retract her request, Peter anxiously answered, "Sure! Sure! But, I've gotta meet someone after school, for like, twenty minutes or so. But I could meet you after that."

Nicola's impatient friends were staring daggers at her from just outside the classroom door. "Cool," she said. "So, uh, just come to my place when you're done. At say, like, four or so? Thanks, Pete. I owe you one."

Peter noticed that his heart was now racing and his palms were cold and sweaty. Even though he knew Nicola was only looking for a way to get her homework done quickly, deep down he hoped he could find some way to get her to become his girlfriend.

Not wanting to waste any time, Peter stuffed everything in his backpack and bolted out the door. He wanted to get through his meeting with the old man as quickly as possible. He had to make sure he wouldn't be even a minute late to get to Nicola's after.

CHAPTER 8

At three fifteen, Peter arrived at the arranged meeting place, the area near the *Welcome to Clearville: Population 4500* sign on the highway into town. The old man was supposed to be waiting there for Peter, but hadn't arrived yet. Peter looked around as he walked through the dirt and tall grass, wondering which direction the old man would come in from.

"Why on earth does he wanna meet me on the side of the highway?" Peter asked himself. "There's absolutely nothing here."

"And the fact that there is nothing here," the old man suddenly said, catching Peter completely by surprise, "is precisely why I chose it."

Peter quickly spun around to face the old man. He was definitely not there five seconds ago. It was as if he had appeared there out of thin air.

"How did you...?" Peter said, in complete and utter shock. "What are you? Some sort of magician?"

"C'mon Peter," the old man laughed. "We both know magic isn't real. It's just smoke and mirrors. Please don't disappoint me by saying you can't figure out where I was."

Since Peter was quite proud of his ability to solve things, he quickly began thinking. He scanned the area nearby the old man, and his mind raced through all of the various possibilities. One by one, he quickly eliminated the improbable ones.

Before sixty seconds had elapsed, he had pieced it together. Peter pointed towards the long and narrow mirror which was lying face down in the dirt and grass. The old man had obviously been holding up the mirror and hiding behind it.

"You were doing nothing more than just standing behind a mirror," Peter said. "And since the terrain around here all looks the same, the reflection of the ground in the mirror blended in with the surroundings perfectly. You were hiding behind the mirror while I walked down the road."

Peter stood proudly with his hands on his hips, and continued, "So am I right, or am I right?"

The old man starting applauding, but with very long and slow claps. He was not congratulating Peter on a job well done, but instead seemed to be mocking him. Peter became quite irritated, and took a few steps closer to the old man.

"What's your problem?" Peter asked him. "You said you needed me to solve puzzles, right? And I just did. And now you're laughing at me?"

The old man didn't even flinch, but simply returned Peter's glare. "On a scale of one to ten," he said, "with ten being very difficult, this silly little trick of mine would be... let's say... a two. Only a two!"

Now both angry and confused, Peter threw his arms up in the air. "Stop right there!" he yelled at the old man. "Silly little trick?! Two out of ten?! What on earth are you talking about? Look, I think I've played along with your games for long enough. Either you tell me exactly what's going on, or I'll run to the nearest house I can find and call the cops. I'll tell them some weird old guy is wandering around and scaring kids."

The old man sighed and put his wrinkled hands in his pockets. He looked slowly up to the sky, and then back at Peter. "Alright," he said calmly. "I owe you an explanation. Peter, this is not about me. Nor is it about playing silly games. It's not a game at all. It's actually very, very serious. I need your help. No, let me rephrase that. *We* need your help. And by we, I mean everyone. So let me start from the—"

"Hold up!" Peter replied, cutting the old man off. "I'll be honest with you too. I like the fact that you are into puzzles. I've never met anyone who likes them as much as me. But solving puzzles and being *needed by everyone* are two completely different things."

The old man stayed quiet, waiting for Peter to continue.

"But when we met this morning," Peter said, "I promised you I'd hear you out. So hurry up and tell me your story, before I change my mind."

They walked a few meters to a place where there were some piles of dirt large enough to sit down on. Peter motioned for the man to sit down first, and then sat beside him.

CHAPTER 9

"I'll try to make this as short and simple as possible," the old man said. "But it won't make sense unless I explain everything, from start to finish.

"You have obviously noticed the awful storms that have been occurring more and more frequently recently. And you are probably aware that meteorologists, from all over the world, have been unable to come up with any explanation about what's causing them.

"Well, the laws of nature are actually not the only things that influence the weather. As far-fetched as this may sound, many aspects of weather are controlled by supernatural beings.

"For the sake of simplicity, let's call these supernatural beings *weather gods*. These weather gods are the only reason that life on our planet, and countless other planets, has been able to survive.

"Here's how it works. For each inhabited planet in the universe, one weather god is sent for a span of fifty years. While there, they do everything in their power to limit the devastation that the environment can cause. They change the direction of hurricanes, shorten the length of droughts, and even reduce the magnitude of earthquakes. They use their powers to help keep planets habitable, and ensure the creatures on those plants remain safe.

"But each planet is very different. Most are quite small, and many don't even have seasons. Obviously, those ones are extremely easy to manage. Those are the places that all weather gods hope to go to. It's like a fifty-year holiday, where they rarely have to do any work.

"On the other hand, Earth is one of the most challenging and difficult planets to be sent to. Because of its size and the complexity of the environment here, it's unbelievably hard to manage.

"Earth's current weather god is named Zoltan Screed XVI. Zoltan is very young, well at least as far as weather gods go. And Earth is his first assignment. However, Zoltan never expected to be sent here.

"Zoltan is quite clever, but incredibly lazy. And Zoltan knew how the planet assignments were made. He knew that once every fifty years, the twelve lead weather gods held an anonymous vote in a secluded chamber. They wrote their votes on small pieces of paper, put them in a special box, and the votes would be counted the following morning.

"So Zoltan snuck into the chamber at night and changed some of the names. But he was caught. And as a punishment, he was assigned to Earth.

Since it was a punishment, Zoltan put very little effort into his work. He quickly noticed that when he did very little, the weather caused horrific damage. And in a very sick way, he felt some sort of satisfaction watching the people of Earth suffer."

The old man paused. For the last few minutes, Peter had seemed very distracted.

"Peter," he said, "you clearly have somewhere else you want to be, don't you?"

"What do you mean?" Peter replied.

"You have looked at your watch seven times since I began telling this story. Seven times. School is out for the day, and you're too young to work. So my best guess is that you are going to meet someone. Probably a girl, right?"

Peter tried to hide his embarrassment, but the old man had just hit the nail on the head.

"My story is nowhere near finished," the old man said, "but I have a better idea."

The old man reached into his small bag and

pulled out a DVD.

"Take this home," he said to Peter while handing it to him. "Watch it. I never expected someone like you to believe any of this without some kind of proof. Well, this is your proof. If it convinces you, then come back here at the same time tomorrow."

Peter quickly put it into his bag. "OK," he replied, checking his watch again.

"Now off you go to your girl!" the old man said. "But remember to watch the DVD! Tonight!"

"Don't worry," Peter answered quickly while running to his bike, "I will!"

It was only 3:37. He'd easily make it to Nicola's before four o'clock.

But while riding towards her house, he didn't feel the anticipation and nervousness that he usually did before talking to Nicola. Instead, he couldn't stop thinking about the amazing story he had just heard.

"Worry about that later," he said to himself. "Don't blow your chance with Nik!"

CHAPTER 10

Time at Nicola's went by way too fast. He spent just over an hour helping her out with math and joking around. Hanging out with Nicola seemed so easy and natural when her new friends weren't around.

As he rode home, he tried to convince himself that one day Nicola would ditch her new friends and become his girlfriend. He already knew all of the places they would hang out together.

He got home just before five thirty. Surprisingly, no one else was back yet. His mom and dad were probably busy at work and had to stay later than usual. And he figured that Bradley and Sophia were most likely with friends.

"Lucky!" he said to himself. He knew this was his chance to watch the DVD the old man had given him, as he wouldn't be able to if anyone else was home.

He took the DVD out of his backpack and put it

on the coffee table. He wasn't exactly sure how he felt about watching it. The whole idea of a supernatural being destroying the world by altering the weather was absolutely preposterous. Peter had a scientific mind, and would only believe claims supported by evidence and facts. But despite all of his doubts, he couldn't deny his intrigue.

"Well, here goes nothing," he said while putting it into the DVD player.

The video began with the old man standing next to the *Welcome to Clearville* sign. It was exactly the same place Peter had met him earlier that afternoon. The camera was completely still, so Peter guessed that the old man had set it up on a tripod or something.

> *"This video is being shot with one camera," the old man said, "which will run the whole time, without being stopped. Trust me, there will be no camera tricks."*
>
> *About thirty or forty meters behind the old man, a tall man wearing a hooded cloak walked in from the left.*
>
> *"The man standing back there is Zoltan," the old man said. "He may not look scary, but let me assure you that what you are about to see will terrify*

you. Anyways, let's start the demonstration. As you can see, Zoltan is standing over there, by himself, in the middle of the field. And it's exactly noon. If you don't believe me, look at the shadow being cast by the population sign. The weather is clear and sunny, which you can obviously see for yourself."

The old man then turned around and yelled to Zoltan, "Zoltan, a demonstration please! How about a... a sudden storm! Rain, wind, thunder, lightning, the works! But take it easy on the hail. I don't want the camera to break."

Zoltan nodded his head and lifted his arms into the air. He yelled something up at the sky, but it wasn't in any language that Peter was familiar with. Zoltan kept looking upwards, as if he were ordering the sky to do something.

Within seconds, huge black clouds filled the sky. A powerful wind immediately followed the clouds. Then the loud and heavy rain started.

Peter's jaw dropped. Less than a minute earlier, he had been looking at a clear and sunny day. Now he was watching an intense storm. It was impossible. It was absolutely, completely impossible. But the camera had never stopped. There were no tricks. So what had just happened?

"That's enough Zoltan!" the old man said.

Zoltan lowered his arms and looked ahead again. The rain and wind died down within seconds, and the clouds quickly vanished.

The old man, soaked by the storm, walked up closer to the camera.

"That is just a small portion of what Zoltan is capable of," he said. "He can do anything he wants with the weather."

The old man turned around to face Zoltan again. "Let's see a tornado!" he said. "I want to make sure Peter is one hundred percent convinced! But not too close by. Do it over there somewhere, where nothing will get damaged."

Just like before, Zoltan raised his arms and began mumbling incoherently at the sky. About twenty seconds later, an enormous tornado formed about one or two kilometers away from them.

"Hold on, Peter," the old man said. "Let me zoom in the camera so you can

get a better look."

As the camera zoomed in on the tornado, it became clear that this was the real thing. And it wasn't just any tornado. It was a very, very strong one.

Peter went to pick up the remote so he could stop the DVD, but it slipped right out of hand and fell back on the coffee table. The mix of excitement and fear had made his hands sweat like crazy.

Zoltan then stopped the tornado, and the old man approached the camera once more.

"A picture is worth a thousand words," *he said. "Meet me again tomorrow, and I'll finish my story."*

CHAPTER 11

The next day at school, Peter kept replaying in his mind what he had seen on the DVD. He was still trying to wrap his head around the fact that supernatural beings existed. He couldn't decide if he was more amazed or more terrified. Peter wished he had his own supernatural power right now, so he could use to it to speed the clock up to three o'clock.

But Peter would have to wait. Wait and wait and wait, until the clock slowly ticked its way to the final bell of the day.

When it finally did, Peter made a beeline for door. He was the first kid out of the front doors of the school, and was on his bike less than ninety seconds after the bell had rung.

* * *

The old man was standing beside the sign when Peter rode up. Huffing and puffing from how hard he had pedaled, he jumped off his bike, and let it fall to the ground. "I'm all ears," Peter said.

The old man took a deep breath and looked at the curiosity in Peter's eyes. He knew he would have Peter's full attention for the remainder of the tale.

"As you saw clearly in the video," the old man began, "Zoltan can use the weather to do anything he pleases. But his sick and twisted mind led him to *cause* destruction instead of prevent it. He started playing some kind of game with himself, where he tried to make each new storm stronger than the previous one. The more powerful he made them, the more people suffered. And the more they suffered, the more he enjoyed it.

"And that's where I came into the picture. I joined together with representatives from numerous other countries, and we pleaded for mercy. We offered Zoltan anything he wanted. Any extravagance he could imagine. Unfortunately, material goods were of no interest to him.

"Thankfully, he did provide us with one window of opportunity. He said that he would stop the destruction, his only form of entertainment, if we could provide him with an equally satisfying entertainment. Believe it or not, games and puzzles were that entertainment. And since I was the best at making challenging ones, Zoltan selected me to be the one to create his puzzles. As long as I filled Zoltan's days by providing him with challenging new games and puzzles, he left the people of earth alone.

"But Peter, this started over twenty-five years ago. Look at me now. I'm old. For the last couple years, my mind hasn't been what it once was. Zoltan's boredom with my substandard puzzles over the last two years has caused him to go back to the only other form of entertainment he knows, causing destruction by messing with the weather.

"I need someone to replace me. I've been searching for ages. For over half a year. And finally, I've found my replacement. You."

"Your replacement?" Peter answered in disbelief.

"Exactly," the old man said. "You can take over for me. You can become the one who makes the puzzles. And then Zoltan will stop causing all of these storms. People will be safe again."

Peter was speechless. He was overwhelmed. But before he could respond, he needed some time to think.

"Sleep on it," the old man said, as if he had just read Peter's mind. "Come back tomorrow and tell me your decision."

CHAPTER 12

The next day after school, Peter went to meet the old man again. The ball was in Peter's court now, so the old man waited patiently for Peter to speak first. But in his mind, he already knew what Peter was about to say.

"I'll do it," Peter said.

The man approached Peter with a smile and shook his hand. "Well, first things first," the old man said. "Allow me to formally introduce myself. I'm Leonardo Alexander Winchester."

"So you do have a name," Peter joked. "Nice to meet you, Mr. Winchester."

"The pleasure is all mine," Mr. Winchester responded. "And I look forward to getting to know you better. But first, let me tell you some good news. I actually met with Zoltan last night. And I told him I was ninety-nine percent sure I had found my replacement."

"And how did he react?" Peter asked. "I bet he

laughed his head off."

"Actually, he was quite excited by the idea," Mr. Winchester said. "But he will only allow you to replace me if you can solve a series of puzzles. And Zoltan himself will create them. He will make eight puzzles for you, and each one will be harder than the previous one. If you can solve all eight, then you will officially replace me. And the date for these challenges has been set. Exactly fifty days from today."

"Fifty days?" Peter replied, not sure if that was a long time or a short time.

"And I managed to get him to agree to two terms," Mr. Winchester continued. "Both of which will help our preparations go more smoothly. Number one: He has agreed to cause no more destruction for the next fifty days. And number two: He has agreed to allow you to recruit three people to join you."

"Join me?" Peter blurted out, feeling a little offended.

Mr. Winchester looked Peter directly in the eyes, wanting to make sure that he had Peter's complete attention. "You are exceptionally clever," he said. "There's no arguing that. But different types of puzzles require different types of skills. Not all of them are solved by brains only."

"I'm not following you," Peter replied, fairly confused.

"Well let me explain it this way," Mr. Winchester continued. "Some puzzles will require more than just intelligence. Some might need strength. Some might need patience. Some might even need things that one person could not do on their own. So you see, you *need* a team."

"A team?!" Peter said. "How and where am I going to find people so quickly? It took you forever to find me. What do you expect me to do? Ask people from school? Ask my relatives?"

Mr. Winchester crossed his arms behind his back and took a deep breath.

"That, Peter," he said, "is precisely who you will ask."

"And how do you propose I persuade them to help me?" Peter said, still quite frustrated.

"I can promise you one thing," Mr. Winchester replied, giggling a little. "Getting three people to join you will be, by far, the easiest part of what lays ahead. So off you go. Once you have assembled your team, the training can begin."

CHAPTER 13

Peter woke up at the crack of dawn the next morning. He looked at the list of potential candidates he had tried to write the night before. He had three columns on his list, one for each of the three types of people he was looking for. He wanted one person with strength, one who was very careful and precise, and one who could think out of the box. He had written four or five names in each column.

He picked up a pen and started crossing off any people he thought would refuse his request. That left him with only two or three in each column. Then he went through the remaining names one by one, thinking about how well he really knew each person.

More quickly than expected, Peter was down to only one name in each row. He had Bradley for *strength*, Nicola for *careful and precise*, and Neil under *think outside of the box*.

Peter figured it was going to be easy to get Neil on board. Even though Neil seemed to always be in his own little world, Peter considered him a close friend. Neil had the habit of talking about the weirdest things at the oddest times, so he was regularly teased by other kids. Peter was also the target of teasing, so they had formed some sort of bond.

* * *

Peter left home eight minutes earlier than usual, and was now waiting just around the corner from Neil's house.

A few minutes later, the front door opened and Neil walked out, carrying nothing but his lunch bag. When he was almost at the end of his driveway, the door opened again. Neil's mom ran down the driveway and gave Neil his backpack. Peter guessed that this kind of thing probably happened a lot.

Whistling happily as he walked, Neil was heading straight to where Peter was standing. But since Neil wasn't paying attention to anything around him, he hadn't noticed Peter at all.

"Hey, man. What's up?" Peter said, trying not to startle or surprise him.

After finally noticing Peter, Neil responded, "What are you doing here? Your house is the other way."

Peter knew Neil wasn't being rude. This was

just another example of how he often spoke before thinking.

"I just thought we could walk in together today," said Peter.

Neil made no attempt to answer Peter. He also showed no expression about whether or not he was happy to walk to school together with someone for a change.

Peter started the speech he had rehearsed earlier. "You remember when you brought your yo-yo to school last week?" he said. "And you did all of those cool tricks? Well, I was up in the attic yesterday, and guess what? I found some old yo-yos up there. I brought one with me. I thought you could check it out and tell me what you think."

"A yo-yo?" Neil replied enthusiastically. "Sure! Let's see it. I wonder if it's a ball bearing one or not? I doubt it, since it's old."

Peter had no idea what Neil was talking about, but he played along. He pulled the yo-yo out of his backpack and handed it to Neil. "Here it is," he said. "What do you make of it? Is it usable? Or should we just throw it out?"

"Wow!" Neil replied excitedly. "This is old school! People stopped using this type, like, five or six years ago." Neil unwound the string and looked at it carefully. "The string is frayed. But if I change it, it should work. Hold on, I think I've got some extras in my bag."

Neil squatted down and opened up his overstuffed backpack. He started digging through it to find a yo-yo string.

"I left the other yo-yos at home," Peter said. "But you can have them too if you want. Why don't you come over after school today? You can check them out. If want them, they're all yours."

"Really? Are you sure?" Neil replied.

Of course, Peter didn't really have any more yo-yos at home. He just needed an excuse to get Neil to come over.

CHAPTER 14

Peter had trouble paying attention to anything at school for the entire day. He had been continuously rehearsing how to approach Nicola. The final bell of the day was going to ring in just over four minutes, so his nerves were causing his palms and armpits to sweat profusely.

"Chill out," he whispered to himself. He kept reminding himself to stick to the plan.

As soon as the bell started to ring, Peter jumped from his seat and walked directly over to Nicola. She had only just started to put the first of her books in her bag.

"Hey Nik," Peter said, trying to mask his nervousness. "You know that big biology project that's due next month? Mr. Wittbaker said we can do it alone or in pairs, right? Do you wanna go with me? I mean... I'll like... do most of the research. You could be in charge of making the poster."

"Really?" Nicola replied happily, clearly realizing that the offer was a generous one. She knew she would get an *A* if she did the project with Peter. "Yeah, sure," she said with a smile. "But, you know, I'm not so good at science."

"Don't worry," Peter replied. "So... can you come over to my place at four or so today? I'll show you what I've done so far. And I'll explain about the poster and stuff."

"Yeah, no problem," Nicola said as she started towards the door. "First math help and now science. You're the best!"

So both Neil and Nicola were now set to come over to Peter's place after school. The first part of his plan had worked.

CHAPTER 15

Peter rode home as quickly as he could, getting back at 3:17. He needed to have the house to himself when Nicola and Neil arrived. His parents would still be at work, and Bradley had basketball practice today, so that only left Sophia to deal with.

Peter had a simple and clever plan to get Sophia out of the house for a while. At three forty-five, he went up to her room and said he had a favor to ask. He told his sister he really felt like a chocolate bar, but was too lazy to ride all the way to the convenience store to buy one. If she would ride there and buy one for him, then he'd give her enough money to buy some stuff for herself too.

Sweets were few and far between at their house, so she gladly accepted. Peter knew the trip there and back, at her speed, would take at least forty-five minutes.

* * *

Neil rang the doorbell just before four o'clock, and Nicola got there shortly after. Peter didn't have much time to waste, so he got right to the point.

"Look guys," he said, "the real reason I asked you over today has nothing to do with yo-yos or a biology poster."

"What do you mean?" asked Nicola.

"C'mon, follow me," Peter said, leading them into the family room.

Peter had already set up the DVD, so all he had to do was press play. And after it finished, he retold the story he had heard from Mr. Winchester. He tried to cover all of the important points as quickly as possible.

Peter had expected a lot of questions, but got none. They both appeared overwhelmed by the seriousness of what they had just seen and heard. Before Peter even had a chance to ask them if they would help or not, they told him they wanted in. It was almost like they felt they really had no choice. They had just seen what would happen if they didn't try to help.

"But I haven't asked Brad yet," Peter said.

"Brad?" Nicola said excitedly. "Is Brad going to be on our team too?"

Peter had heard the girls at school talking about his *cool and sexy* older brother. Apparently Nicola was also one of his adoring fans. But Peter would have to deal with that later.

"I think I have a plan about asking Brad," Peter said. "I'm going to tell him that we are training for some kind of big athletic competition, and that we want him on our team. I'll tell him it's a really big one, and that people from all over the country will come to compete. Knowing Brad, he'll jump at the chance to enter something like that. There's nothing he loves more than winning something and then bragging about it."

"But what if he checks it out and finds out it's not real?" Nicola asked.

"I know how to fool him," said Neil. "My cousin, the one in university, is majoring in media and design. He could create a believable poster in his sleep! He's got all of the software on his computer at home. I'm sure he'd do it for us. Well, if we pay him, I mean. And if we pay him enough, I bet he'd make a fake website too, just in case Brad tries to check it out online."

Peter gave Neil a high-five.

"Awesome plan!" Peter said. "But how long will it take?"

"For the right price, I can get him to do it tonight," Neil answered.

Peter ran upstairs. He had a hidden stash of money in his sock drawer, which he had earned from delivering newspapers and mowing lawns.

"OK, here's all the money I've got," he said.

"There must be least fifty or sixty bucks in total. But don't offer it all right away. Start at like twenty or so. And if that's not enough, keep offering more and more."

"Cool," Neil replied. "He'll probably go for twenty, but we'll see. Anyway, you just leave it to *the Neilster.*"

Neil went to the front door and started tying up his shoes. Once he was out the door, he turned around and yelled, "I'll be back with your poster before you go to bed!"

CHAPTER 16

The next morning, poster in hand, Peter walked out of his room and down the stairs. When he got to the kitchen, Bradley was alone at the table. The bowl of cornflakes in front of Bradley was big enough for at least three people.

"How's it going?" Peter said.

Bradley responded with only a grunt, and then went back to stuffing his face with cereal.

"Hey Brad," Peter said, sitting down on the other side of the table. "I gotta ask you something."

"No, you can't borrow my bike," Bradley replied coldly, without even looking up from his food. "I'm going to Jason's house after school today, and you know how far away he lives."

"I don't wanna use your bike," Peter said quickly. "Actually, I need your help."

"My help?" Bradley laughed, causing some cornflakes to spray from his mouth. "With what?"

"There's a new outdoor sporting competition," Peter said. "It's called the *Brains and Brawn Championship*. Actually, I've already signed us up for it. I figured since you are the strongest guy in school, and I am the smartest, we could win it in a breeze."

"The what?" Bradley said. "Never heard of it."

"You haven't?" Peter asked. "What about all of the posters that are up all over town?"

Peter unfolded the poster and put it on the table in front of Bradley. Neil's cousin had done a great job. It looked very authentic.

"Like I said, it's new," Peter continued. "It's a pretty big thing, too. It's a national competition."

Bradley looked more intrigued now. "You mean reporters will be there and, like, interview us and stuff?" he asked.

"You got it!" Peter answered. "Well, I mean, as long as we win."

Bradley held up his hand to Peter for a high-five. "Petey, my friend," he said. "You know I never lose. This will be a piece of cake."

Peter gave Bradley the high-five he had been waiting for, and then sat down and poured himself a bowl of cornflakes. Their little white lie had worked perfectly.

CHAPTER 17

At three forty-five that afternoon, Neil came over to Peter's home. Shortly after, Bradley walked out of the house to join them on the front porch. Peter spent a few minutes lying to Bradley about how each four-person team in the *Brains and Brawn Championship* was required to have one girl.

A couple minutes past four o'clock, they watched as Nicola casually walked up the driveway. "Hey Pete, hey Neil," she said while starting up the stairs. Then she saw Bradley sitting behind them. She greeted him in a completely different tone, "Hi, Brad. Remember me?"

Bradley smiled, but didn't say anything back.

Nicola then sat down beside Bradley, and tossed her hair to one side. "C'mon Brad," she said. "You remember me, don't you? You used to pull my pigtails and make me cry."

This comment made all three boys laugh a

little.

"Well look at me now!" she continued, standing up and twirling around once. "Sure have grown up, haven't I?"

Bradley watched as Nicola posed in front of them as if she were in a fashion show. "You're gonna be popular when you get to high school," he said. "You're already hotter than most of the chicks there now!"

"Oh?" Nicola giggled, still trying to appeal to Bradley. "C'mon... Now you're teasing!"

Peter stood up and turned around to face everyone. He reminded them that the date of the competition was only seven weeks away. When Nicola heard Peter say that they would be practicing regularly for the next seven weeks, which would mean countless hours around Bradley, she looked like she had just won the lottery.

"This competition is going to be a lot harder than we think," Peter said at the end of his little speech. "But if prepare well, I think we have a good shot at winning. We start training tomorrow morning. Be at the entrance of Meeks Park at ten. Mr. Winchester will be waiting there for us."

When Peter finally crawled into bed at around midnight, he couldn't stop worrying about how long his crazy lie to Bradley would hold up. When would he have to tell Bradley the truth? And how would he tell him?

CHAPTER 18

The following day, which was Saturday, Peter intentionally arrived at Meeks Park twenty minutes early. He needed a chance to talk to Mr. Winchester before Bradley got there. Mr. Winchester had already arrived, and was setting up some folding chairs under a large tree.

"Before Brad gets here," Peter said hurriedly, "there's something important I need to tell you. In order to put this team together on such short notice, I had to... uh... tell a couple of little white lies."

"Little white lies?" Mr. Winchester responded.

Peter spent the next ten minutes giving a rushed explanation about how Bradley was under the impression that they were preparing for a competition. Mr. Winchester listened carefully to the whole story.

"So you have to go along with it," Peter said at the end of his explanation, "or else he'll quit. And I don't know anyone who could take his spot."

Mr. Winchester nodded his head a few times, and then replied, "I see. Although I'm going to be training your team, you are the leader of it. If you want me to play along with this lie, then that's what I'll do."

"OK," Peter said, not really sure what else to say. "Thanks."

"No need for thanks," Mr. Winchester said back quickly. "It is *I* who should be thanking *you*. If you had turned down my request, then Zoltan would—"

"Hey Pete!" a voice called from behind them. "Didn't you say ten? You're early, aren't you?"

They spun around and saw Neil standing there, wearing baggy shorts and an oversized T-shirt. As Neil approached, he put out his hand to Mr. Winchester.

"You must be the super old dude that Peter said is going to train us," Neil said while shaking Mr. Winchester's hand. "Oh, by the way, I'm Neil."

Peter hung his head and looked at the ground. He couldn't believe the ridiculous comment that had just come out of Neil's mouth.

"Young Neil," Mr. Winchester said politely. "I am indeed the person who will be training you. But what exactly is a *super old dude*?"

Neil giggled, and took a seat on one of the folding chairs.

Very shortly after, Bradley came roaring towards them on his mountain bike. He pulled the back brake hard, causing the back wheel to lock and kick up dust as he ground to a halt just a couple of meters away. He looked at his watch and triumphantly announced, "Made it here in less than six minutes! I guarantee you won't find anyone else this fast in the entire town!"

Mr. Winchester stepped forward and shook Bradley's hand. "You must be Bradley," he said. "Peter has told me a lot about you. With you on this team, we can surely..." Mr. Winchester paused suddenly, as if he were uncomfortable about what he was going to say next. "Win this... this... competition."

"You bet, dude," Bradley answered, shaking Mr. Winchester's hand so hard that Peter thought he was going to pull the old man's shoulder out of its socket.

"So I guess we are just waiting for Pete's sweetheart to show up now, right?" Neil said.

Peter's ears instantly turned red. Even though most of the other kids in grade seven knew about his crush on Nicola, Bradley certainly didn't. Now it had just become public knowledge.

"Oh, so she's your little girlfriend then, is she?" Bradley asked in a sarcastic tone. "Well, I guess she must be a lot geekier than she looks."

Before Peter could figure out how to respond,

they all spotted Nicola walking their way. She was arriving fashionably late by about five minutes. And her outfit and make-up today made her look at least sixteen years old.

Being the only gentlemen in the group, Mr. Winchester walked up to greet her as she approached. "Young lady," he said. "If your mind is even a fraction of your beauty, then you will be the secret weapon that will propel this team to victory."

Nicola felt her cheeks turn a shade of pink. She was hoping that Bradley didn't notice, as she was trying to maintain her *cool and casual* look.

"It's a pleasure to meet you, Nicola," Mr. Winchester continued, lightly shaking her hand.

Nicola sat down on the remaining seat, and Mr. Winchester stood in front of them. "I'm not going to waste your time," he said. "And I'm not going to try to make this sound easier than it is. This competition is going to be very, very hard. You may all look confident right now, but without the proper training and practice, you won't have a chance. You either do this right, or you don't do it at all."

Peter, Nicola, Neil, and Bradley looked back and forth at each other. None of them spoke, which meant they all agreed to take this seriously. But they had no clue how hard their training was going to be.

CHAPTER 19

Their first two weeks of training went by in a flash. They were meeting on Tuesday and Thursday afternoons, plus all day on Saturdays and Sundays. Mr. Winchester had created a training regime that covered the skills he figured they needed the most. They worked on strength and endurance, calculation, perception, and teamwork.

The strength and endurance training was extremely hard for everyone except Bradley. Mr. Winchester explained that some of the challenges would involve some type of pushing, pulling, running, jumping, or lifting. Bradley knew this was his forte, and he loved showing off as much as he could while training. He was always the first to finish any race, and he could lift more than Peter, Neil, and Nicola combined.

"Bradley, Bradley, Bradley," Mr. Winchester said one day after Bradley had finished an obstacle course before the rest were even half-done.

"You are built like an ox, but you can run like the wind." This comment, and other similar ones, made Bradley beam with pride.

The calculation training was a breeze for Peter, but was not going so well for the rest of the team. In one of their first calculation training sessions, they were given a pile of thirty small metal blocks, all different sizes and weights. The task was to divide them up into three piles of exactly equal weight. And it had to be performed without the use of any type of scale. Less than thirty seconds after starting, Bradley threw his arms up in defeat and sat on the ground.

"Out of my league!" he announced. "Pete, you got this one. I'll save my energy for the ones that require some strength."

Right after Bradley said that, Mr. Winchester suddenly grabbed Peter's left arm and twisted it behind his back.

"Ouch! Let go!" Peter screamed. "How do you expect me to solve this puzzle when it feels like you're gonna break my arm in half?"

"Let go of my brother, old man!" Bradley yelled, standing up and coming towards Mr. Winchester. "Or I'll pound the crap out of you!"

Mr. Winchester had no intention of hurting Peter, so he let go and spun around to look at Bradley. "We all know Peter is good at these kinds of things," he said in a stern voice. "But as you just witnessed, he was completely useless when I distracted him. You can't depend on him all the time. If Peter loses his concentration, or gets hurt or something during one of the challenges, what are you going to do? Give up? Quit?"

Bradley was fuming. It looked as if he was ready to punch Mr. Winchester in the face. "Look, old man," he said.

Mr. Winchester was also quite upset now, so he quickly responded, "Don't *look old man* me Bradley. I am preparing you so that you can win this thing. If you are planning to give up whenever something looks a little too hard for you, then you have no hope of winning. We don't need any quitters on this team."

Mr. Winchester then walked over to one of the nearby park benches and sat down.

Nicola had been silent throughout the entire ordeal, but she decided to speak up. "I think someone better go and apologize to him," she said. "He wasn't trying to break anyone's arm or make anyone feel stupid. He just wants us to win. Think about how hard it must be to try to teach all of this stuff to us."

"She's right," said Neil, without thinking through how silly his next comment was going to sound. "He's the best coach that money can buy."

"OK, I'll do it," Bradley said first. "I suppose I started this. I'll go fix it."

The others watched as Bradley walked over and sat beside Mr. Winchester. No one could hear what was being said, but less than three minutes after sitting down, Bradley and Mr. Winchester shook hands. Then they both stood up and walked back to the group.

CHAPTER 20

The perception training was their biggest challenge, as none of the four truly understood what or how they were supposed to practice.

In one of the early training sessions, Mr. Winchester asked Neil to open his hand. "OK, let's practice perception for a while," he said to them.

"Dice?" Neil replied, as Mr. Winchester dropped them into his hand.

"The task is very simple," Mr. Winchester continued. "Roll these two until you get a total of seven. That's it."

Neil looked at the other three, not really knowing what to say. He shrugged his shoulders and shook the dice in his hand. Then he rolled them on the ground.

"Did you do it?" Mr. Winchester asked.

Neil looked at the dice. "No," he replied. "I rolled a six and a two, for a total of eight."

"Good math, Einstein," Bradley joked.

"Shut up, Brad!" Neil said back quickly.

Peter jumped in, "C'mon guys. Rolling dice is simply about odds. The odds of rolling a seven are one in six. If you roll six times or more, it's highly likely one of them will be a seven. Neil, pass me those."

Peter rolled a pair of twos. On his second try, he rolled a ten.

Bradley snatched the dice out of Peter's hand before his third attempt. "You guys have no luck," he said. "Leave it to a *real* man to roll a seven."

Bradley rolled an eight. He tried again, but still couldn't get a seven. "Third time lucky!" he proudly announced, holding the dice high above his head.

"You should just give up!" Nicola said loudly. "I guarantee you will not roll a seven this time, or the next time, or the time after that."

"And how could you, little girl, possibly know this?" Bradley asked sarcastically.

"Because if you look closely at those dice," she replied, "you'll see there are no odd numbers on them. They only have twos, fours, and sixes. So you'll never, ever get a total of seven."

Bradley twirled the dice around in his fingers. Once he realized what Nicola was saying was true, he turned to Mr. Winchester and said, "You tricked us, old man! These aren't real dice."

"I most certainly did *not* trick you," Mr.

Winchester replied firmly. "If you recall, I put two objects into Neil's hand. And I did not call them dice. It was Neil, followed quickly by the rest of you, who made that assumption."

"That's still pretty tricky though," Neil added, a little flustered about his mistake.

Peter was hoping to put a stop to what seemed like the start of a tense moment. "Calm down, guys," he said. Unfortunately, he hadn't spoken as boldly or loudly as he should have. It appeared as if this argument was going to escalate.

Nicola was the only one still seated. She uncharacteristically yelled, "Shut up and sit down! It seems to me like you *boys* have had your pride hurt by a *girl*. You guys are pathetic. Think about what happened? Before giving those two dice to Neil, Mr. Winchester said we were going to work on perception. Perception! If you had been listening, you would have known to look more carefully at the dice, instead of just rolling them over and over."

The boys sat back down. They were shocked by Nicola's sudden character change, and also embarrassed by their careless mistake.

Mr. Winchester cleared his throat and then announced, "Thank you Nicola. I can see you will be needed to keep these boys honest. And boys, let this be a lesson to all of you. We all have weaknesses. I can only hope that all four of you don't share a common one."

"Why are you lecturing *me*?" Bradley asked in an angry tone. "I'm the muscle on this team. Not the brains. I'll leave the geeky stuff to these three."

"Who are you calling geeky?" Neil said, standing up and taking a step toward Bradley.

Bradley stood up too. "You, you geek!" he replied. "And Petey and his little geeky girlfriend!"

Peter needed to do something to calm everyone down. But he was too late, as Neil had already pushed Bradley hard in the chest. Bradley didn't fall, but had to take a couple of steps back to keep his balance.

Once Bradley was standing up straight again, he walked towards Neil. Just before he got close enough to hit him, Nicola jumped between them. "STOP!" she screamed at the top of her lungs. "Please just stop!"

Despite how badly he wanted to throw a punch, Bradley wasn't going to risk hitting a girl to try to get at Neil. Peter seized the opportunity and quickly said, "Look, I don't care who's geeky and who isn't. What I care about is winning. C'mon guys. If we spent as much time practicing as we did arguing, we'd be a team to reckon with."

Although this fight had been temporarily averted, Peter wondered how they were going to get through the next six weeks without ripping each other's heads off...

CHAPTER 21

They were now into their third week of training. They had actually made some vast improvements during the first two weeks, but their perception skills were still quite lacking. In an effort to try to help them learn how to notice things better, Mr. Winchester decided to start with a perception challenge today.

He had explained that Zoltan was a big fan of paths, mazes, and *finding the exit* challenges. He wanted them to understand the fact that many of their challenges would require noticing something different than what they thought they were looking for.

Today's perception task was going to help them with this. They were standing at the start of a straight path, about twenty meters or so in length. It was lined with high hedges on both sides. There was a large mirror at the end of the path, with a big red square taped on it. All they had to do was run down the path and touch the red square.

"Peter, give it a go!" Mr. Winchester announced. In the past couple of weeks, the old guy was starting to talk more and more like a teenager.

"Are you sure you can run that far?" Bradley said in a high-pitched voice.

Mr. Winchester turned to Bradley. "We all know you are the fastest," he said. "But this time it's not about speed, it's about perception. C'mon, support your team."

Bradley was a little taken aback by these strong words, but not enough to apologize.

Mr. Winchester looked back at Peter. "There's no starting gun," he said. "You may begin whenever you are ready."

Peter started to run down the path. Actually, it was more of a jog than a run. He was looking all around him to spot the trick that was hidden somewhere in the next twenty meters. He wanted to make sure he didn't step through a tripwire or fall into a camouflaged hole in the ground. His eyes darted everywhere as he slowly and cautiously jogged down the path. He could also see his reflection growing in size, which meant he was running out of time to spot the trick.

"Where's the stupid trap?" Peter asked himself as he jogged past the halfway mark.

He looked back up at his reflection again. He was less than five meters away now, so he could see the red square clearly.

He slowed down a little, and then realized the one place he hadn't checked yet, *up*. "What's going to fall on me, old man?" he said to himself while looking up.

Unfortunately, his upward inspection didn't reveal anything. There was nothing up there other than the blue sky and a few thin clouds.

He was almost at the mirror now, so he slowed to a walk for the final meter and a half. He was just about to put out his hand to touch the red square when his face and his knee simultaneously banged into something. Peter brought up his hands and felt a large, thick pane of glass in front of him. The trick was simpler than he had thought. Mr. Winchester had set a clear pane of glass twenty centimeters in front of the mirror. The trick was that the red square could only be touched if Peter were to move or break the glass.

"OK, I get it," Peter said. "Make sure you always carry supplies, right? Things like a hammer or whatever."

"This challenge can be won without breaking or moving anything," Mr. Winchester answered. "Remember, it's about perception."

Peter was stumped. He had no clue what to do next.

"Allow me to demonstrate," Mr. Winchester said. "Neil, Nicola, Bradley, follow me."

Mr. Winchester, followed by the other three, started walking along the path. About two meters before reaching the end, he stopped and turned to his right. Then he casually walked through a twenty-centimeter gap in the hedge. Shortly after, he reappeared between the glass and the mirror.

"You were too preoccupied looking for a complex trick or trap," he said. "You walked right past the gap without even noticing it. If you look too hard, you'll miss the easy ones."

Peter followed the others through the gap, shaking his head in disappointment.

"Shake it off, Petey," Bradley said while patting him on the shoulder. "I would have run past it too. I bet Neil and Nik would have done the same. Don't beat yourself up."

"Thanks," Peter replied. Unfortunately, Bradley's words of encouragement did little to make Peter feel any better. But at least Bradley was finally offering up some positive comments.

CHAPTER 22

After a long, slow, and boring week of school, it was finally Friday again. Peter couldn't wait for their weekend training to begin. The puzzle solving and camaraderie were becoming more and more fun as time went on. And on top of that, he would get to spend close to twelve hours in the presence of Nicola over the next two days.

Peter ran for the door the instant the bell rang. He was planning to be the first out again today.

"Hold on, Peter," Mrs. Baird said. "I need to talk to you for a minute before you go home."

"Me?" Peter asked, sounding a little irritated.

"Yes, you," she replied sarcastically. "You don't see any other Peters in this room, do you?"

Peter could hear the jocks having a good laugh about that one. "Enjoy your date with the teacher!" he heard from one of them as they left the room.

Peter sat back down at his desk. Once most of the students had left and the room became quieter,

Mrs. Baird approached him.

"Thank you for staying," she said. "Actually, I just wanted to remind you about tomorrow. Remember a few months back when I asked you if you could help tutor math to the weaker students on Saturday mornings?"

Peter recalled the conversation. He also had a feeling about what she was going to say next.

"Well, your name is on the list for tomorrow," she said. "It's only two hours, from nine to eleven. So we'll see you tomorrow morning, Peter. And thank you for volunteering to help."

"OK, Mrs. Baird," Peter replied politely. But inside, he was cursing himself for having agreed to do it in the first place.

Although he was upset that they would have to cancel their morning training tomorrow, he tried to convince himself that being able to train in the afternoon was better than nothing. He would need to phone everyone when he got home to tell them about the change in plans.

Peter got on his bike and started heading home. But as he approached the corner of Beaverbrook Street, a new plan popped into his mind. He would still phone Neil and Mr. Winchester, but decided to drop by Nicola's place and tell her in person. Basically, he had just created a convenient excuse to go and see her.

* * *

He could feel his heart rate speed up as he got closer and closer to Nicola's home. Even though he saw her all the time now, today was different. Neil and Bradley wouldn't be there. This would be the perfect chance to finally ask her out.

The cul-de-sac Nicola lived on was right in front of him, but Peter was way too nervous. He decided to do a big loop through other streets to give his nerves a chance to calm down. He actually ended up doing the loop a total of four times.

Now he was finally ready, and he knew exactly what he was going to say. After telling her about tomorrow, he was going to casually ask her to go out for a movie and dinner next Friday.

"Don't chicken out again," he said to himself, finally riding up to Nicola's house.

He got off his bike and leaned it up against one of the trees in the front yard. He knew Nicola was always outside when it was sunny, so he decided to just walk through to the backyard without ringing the doorbell. If she was in the backyard and he rang the doorbell, she wouldn't be able to hear anyway, right?

When he got to the side of her house, his heart almost stopped. Bradley's bike was leaning up against the side of her house! Peter couldn't believe his eyes. His mind started racing. Was Bradley putting the moves on Nicola? Was he that much of a loser? Or maybe they were secretly going out already, and just hiding it so they wouldn't hurt Peter's feelings.

One thing was for sure. He couldn't be seen by either of them right now. He had to get out of there. But at the same time, he needed a peek at what was going on in the backyard. As quietly as possible, he edged closer and closer to the back of the house.

Just before he got to where he would have been able to see them, he heard Bradley's loud, stupid voice. Peter couldn't make out exactly what Bradley was saying, but it was probably another one of his many stories about how strong or cool he was. And then he heard a happy giggle from Nicola. From the tone of her laugh, Peter deduced that she obviously was crazy about Bradley. They were either already a couple, or were going to be soon.

Peter had heard enough. He tiptoed back to his bike, and quietly pushed it to the end of the cul-de-sac. The he got on and started peddling home in a depressed trance.

When he finally got home, he forced himself to call Neil and Mr. Winchester to tell them about tomorrow. Then he walked upstairs and locked himself in his room.

CHAPTER 23

The next morning, Peter managed to get to tutoring on time, but was literally shaking from how angry he still felt. He looked so flustered and distracted that Mrs. Baird asked him numerous times if everything was OK.

He couldn't believe his backstabbing brother! How could Bradley just come and steal his girlfriend? Well, she wasn't technically his girlfriend yet, but he was getting closer and closer to finally asking her out on a date. But with Bradley in the picture now, everything was ruined! He couldn't compete with Bradley. Bradley was cooler, taller, older, better at sports. He didn't stand a chance.

"Peter?" Mrs. Baird said while lightly tapping him on the shoulder. "If you're not feeling well, that's one thing. But if you do feel fine, then you can't just sit there and ignore everyone's questions. Either help the other students, or go home. You're being very rude to everyone who came here today."

Peter wanted to snap at her, but knew he would regret it later if he did. "I'm sorry, Mrs. Baird," he said. "I barely slept last night, and I have a really bad headache. I want to help, but I just can't seem to concentrate on anything today. Maybe you're right. Maybe I should go home."

"Alright," she replied. "If that's what you feel is best."

"I'm really, really sorry," he repeated. "I promise I'll come in twice next month to make up for today."

Peter left the classroom and started walking down the empty hallway. When he passed Bradley's old locker, number 418, he punched it hard.

"Girlfriend thief!" he yelled, without stopping to see if anyone had seen or heard him.

He got on his bike and started towards Meeks Park. It was only a quarter past ten, so he had almost two hours to figure out what to say to Bradley and Nicola when he got there.

Peter started pedaling harder and harder, until he was going as fast as he could. He saw the turnoff to the park coming up, but since he had no reason to get there this early, he just kept going straight.

"I hate you Brad!" he screamed to the top of his lungs. "I hate you! I hate you!"

* * *

Twenty minutes later, Peter was totally exhausted. He had been riding south on the highway out of town, and was actually pretty close to the neighboring city of Stoneburg now. Plus he was unbelievably thirsty. He knew there was a gas station coming up soon where he could buy himself a soft drink, so he kept heading in the same direction.

A few minutes later, drink in hand, Peter watched the cars roar by on the highway. "Screw them!" he yelled, kicking his bike over intentionally. He had just decided not to go at all today. He was still way, way too angry.

CHAPTER 24

It was almost twelve thirty, so Neil, Nicola, and Bradley had been patiently waiting for Peter at their usual rendezvous point at Meeks Park for quite a while. Mr. Winchester was of course there too, but he was off near the river setting up a few things for training. Everyone was starting to get concerned, as Peter had never been late before.

"What should we do?" Nicola asked the two boys. "Maybe his bike got a flat or something. Why doesn't one of us ride towards his house and see if we can find him?"

"Well I'm definitely the fastest," answered Bradley. "I can make it home and back in, like, twelve minutes or less."

"OK, go for it," Nicola said. "Me and Neil will wait here. But whether you find him or not, make sure you come back right away."

"Be back in a flash!" said Bradley as he mounted his bike. He then put on quite an impressive display of speed as he rode away.

"You know, it's really not like Peter to be late," Nicola said to Neil. "I mean, I've like known him my whole life, and I can't remember him ever not being on time."

"Well there's a first for everything, right?" Neil replied. "But I wouldn't worry. Anyway, Brad will be back before you know it."

* * *

Bradley sizzled down the highway. No sign of Peter anywhere. Then he leaned hard to make the sharp left onto Beaverbrook Street. But Peter was nowhere to be seen. When he skidded to a stop in the driveway, he checked his watch.

"Ladies and Gentlemen!" he announced to the non-existent audience. "I believe we have a new record! Five minutes and twenty-five seconds!"

Peter's bike wasn't in the garage, so Bradley figured that meant he wasn't at home. "I wonder where the little wiener is?" he asked aloud.

* * *

Peter had spent the entire afternoon biking around aimlessly, occasionally stopping here and there to grab a snack or use the washroom. But he made sure to stay clear of any places that Neil, Bradley, or Nicola might come looking for him.

He knew his parents would get angry if he wasn't home for dinner, so he started to head home at about half past five. He ended up arriving home at 5:53, just a few minutes before their regular dinner time.

As he was slowly pushing his bike up the driveway, his mom came running out of the front door. "Peter, we've been worried sick!" she said. "What happened? Are you OK?"

"Huh?" Peter mumbled in reply.

"Nicola came here twice," she continued. "Neil phoned half a dozen times. And Bradley rode all over town looking for you. We were just about to call the police!"

"I'm fine," Peter replied without looking up. He was trying to think up a quick lie to explain his vanishing act.

"You're fine? That's it?" his mom asked angrily.

Peter had thought of his lie. "Actually, after the tutoring," he said, "Mrs. Baird asked if I would mow her lawn for five bucks. Her husband hurt his back or something like that. Anyway, I need the money and I felt a little sorry for her, so I said OK."

Peter's mom didn't reply. She stood with her arms crossed, blocking his path to the door. When Peter finally looked up at her, she could immediately see the distress in his face. Although she knew he was lying through his teeth, something had obviously happened that a young boy wasn't comfortable telling his mom about. She stepped aside and let Peter walk past her into the house.

"And I've got a stomachache," he said while walking upstairs to his room, "so I'm gonna skip dinner."

CHAPTER 25

Peter woke up as early as possible the next morning. He had to make sure he was out of the house well before Bradley got out of bed. He was going to just bike around and kill time, and then show up for their training at exactly ten o'clock. He still didn't know what he was going to say to Nicola and Bradley, even though he'd played through countless scenarios in his mind last night.

He ate and dressed quickly, and then walked out the back door out at 6:52. Was three hours of riding around, with no real place to go, going to be long enough to think?

* * *

When Peter arrived at the park entrance, Neil, Nicola and Bradley were all waiting there for him. Mr. Winchester was sitting on one of the benches by the river.

"You're alive!" Neil yelled, as if he were acting out the scene of a sci-fi movie.

"Pete!" Nicola said while running towards him. She was hugging him even before he had a chance to speak. "Are you OK? I was soooo worried."

"Yeah, man. Me too," said Bradley. "You weird out or something yesterday?"

"Me?" Peter said quietly, stuck for words. It was the first time in his life that Nicola had hugged him. But if she liked Bradley so much, then why was she hugging Peter? Now he was even more confused.

"Anyway," Nicola said, finally releasing her hug after a good ten seconds or so. "You're alright. And that's all that matters!"

"Yeah, I'm cool," Peter replied, feeling re-energized by the big hug.

"And more importantly," Bradley said, "Happy thirteenth!"

Peter had been so busy obsessing about Bradley and Nicola that he had forgotten his own birthday.

"Happy Birthday!" Nicola announced loudly. "Here you go!" She reached in her bag and pulled out a small present.

"We all pitched in," said Bradley. "And then on Friday after school, I went to the mall and bought it. But Nik was worried that I'd lose it before today. You know how messy my room is, right? Anyway, so after I bought it, I went straight to her house to give it to her for safekeeping."

Peter felt ashamed now. Bradley wasn't secretly

dating Nicola at all. The only reason he was at Nicola's house was to drop off Peter's present. Peter had just spent the last forty hours worrying about nothing.

"Open it, man!" yelled Neil. "You're gonna love it!"

Peter ripped off the wrapping paper and opened the small box. It was a brand new digital wristwatch.

"That's quite a nice watch," Mr. Winchester said while he walked over to join the group. "You can test it out right now, as the first part of today's training is a timed challenge."

CHAPTER 26

The next month or so of training went by quickly for everyone, and Mr. Winchester was pleased with their progress. School was now out for summer, so they would be training every day for the final week. They only had six days to go, so Mr. Winchester was giving them harder and harder tasks to try these days. This morning's challenge was going to be their hardest to date.

"Good morning, everyone," Mr. Winchester said. "In order to simulate the real thing, I will be only watching this time. Everything you need for the challenge is in that box over there by the tree, and the instructions are in the envelope pinned to the tree. Good luck."

Mr. Winchester took a few steps back, and sat on a tree stump that would give him a clear view of everything. "And before you ask," he said. "Speed does count, so get a move on it!"

They quickly jogged over to the tree. While

Bradley opened the box, Peter took the envelope off the tree and removed the note inside. He read the notes' contents aloud slowly and clearly.

Object: Get all 6 plastic rings to the opposite side of the river.
Tools: A 5-meter rope, a rock
Rules: Nobody touches the water
Time Limit: 15 minutes

Peter quickly pushed the start button on his new watch. Bradley removed the plastic rings, rope, and rock from the box. Each ring was roughly the size of a dog collar and the thickness of a hot dog. The rope was thick and heavy. And the rock was approximately the size of a baseball. In silence, all four of them looked back and forth between the items and the river in front of them.

Peter estimated the river as being somewhere around ten meters across. It was slightly narrower in a few places, but nowhere was it any less than seven or eight meters wide.

Neil spoke up first. "Brad, you're pretty strong," he said. "Think you could throw them over?"

Bradley tossed one of the rings back and forth between his hands a couple of times. "No way," he said. "They're too light."

Nicola was holding one end of the rope. "And how are we supposed to use the rope?" she asked.

"It's not long enough."

"You aren't supposed to be able to get it right away, Nik." Neil said rudely. "It's called a *challenge*!"

"Shut up, Neil!" Peter said angrily. He didn't have any time to play peacemaker right now. "If you have a suggestion, then speak. Otherwise, keep your mouth shut."

Peter glanced at his watch. Over two minutes had already elapsed.

"Well, I'm pretty sure I could chuck the rock over," Bradley suggested. "It's round, so it'd easy to throw." But after realizing how useless that would be, he put the rock down and looked to Peter for a better idea.

A total of four minutes had gone by, and they still didn't have a feasible plan. Peter picked up the rope and turned towards the other three. "The rope has to hold the answer," he said to them.

"Hey Pete," Neil said a little hesitantly, recalling Peter's comment about when he should and shouldn't speak. "Remember when we were on that camp? And we didn't have enough rope to put up our tarp? Then, Mr. Davidson unwound the rope, and showed us it was actually made of three thinner ropes?"

Peter looked at Neil. "Bingo!" he shouted. "Neil, you start unwinding it. Once you're done, tie the ends together. Then we'll have a fifteen-meter rope."

Peter felt his heartbeat speed up. They were onto something. But they only had nine minutes left. "Think Peter, think," he said to himself. "Figure it out. What are you missing?"

Nicola timidly decided to offer a suggestion. "Pete, there are trees along both sides of the river," she said. "Couldn't we tie it to one of the trees?" But then she realized this wouldn't lead to anything, so she backpedaled. "But wait, I guess that wouldn't help."

Peter turned to face Nicola. "You might be onto something," he said. "Let's roll with it."

Peter's eyes were darting around like mad, trying to spot the solution that hadn't come to mind yet. He kept looking back and forth between the rings, rope and trees.

"Only six more minutes," Nicola said nervously while looking at Peter's watch. "We're running out of time. We gotta try something."

"The rock," Peter said to himself, pacing around in a circle. He picked up the rock and pulled it within inches of his face. "Stupid rock! What am I supposed to do with you?"

And then, like magic, the solution came to him. He turned to Bradley, who was sitting cross-legged on the ground. "Brad, tie one end of the rope to the rock, and then throw it across the river!"

"Why?" Bradley asked. "How's that—"

"Just do it!" Peter yelled, cutting him off.

Slightly over four minutes remained. Peter turned to Neil and said, "Neil, me and you are gonna climb that tree. You hold the rope, and I'll carry the rings."

"Rock tied up Petey!" Bradley said from behind them. "Now watch this sucker fly!"

He threw it with such force that the entire high school baseball team would have been in awe. It easily cleared the river by a few of meters.

"Neil!" Peter yelled impatiently. "C'mon, let's go!"

Neil started up the tree first, with the rope held tightly in one hand. Peter put the rings on his left wrist, and started up behind Neil. Once Neil was about two meters above the ground, Peter said to him, "OK, that should be good enough. The rest of the work will be up to our good old friend, Mr. Gravity."

He carefully passed the rings up to Neil and said, "Neil, put the rings on the rope, and then hold it up as high as you can."

Neil did as instructed. Just as Peter had hoped, the rings were sliding down the rope.

"And whenever they start to slow down," Peter added, "shake the rope a bit, and that will keep them moving."

Neil only had to shake the rope a couple of times, as the rings seemed to be sliding down quite smoothly. In less than a minute, they had slid the entire length of the rope.

The instant the rings reached the other side of the river, Peter glanced at his watch. "Game, set, match!" he yelled in celebration. "And we still have two minutes to spare!"

Down below them, Bradley gave Nicola a high-five. Peter and Neil also joined them for more high-fives as soon as they had made their way back down the tree.

"You're the man!" Bradley said to Peter, pointing at Peter's chest. "The man!"

They all turned around to see Mr. Winchester, who was still sitting on the tree stump. Just as Bradley was about to brag about their performance, Mr. Winchester stood up, and spoke first.

"I am impressed," he said. "You just might have it in you to win this thing." Mr. Winchester looked at his watch, then back at the group. "Let's call it a day. You've earned yourselves an afternoon off. See you tomorrow morning. I'll have something much harder ready."

CHAPTER 27

The next morning, it was clear to Peter and his team that something was wrong. It was twelve minutes past their meeting time, and Mr. Winchester still hadn't arrived. Since he had never been late before, they all started to assume the worst.

Just before ten fifteen, Mr. Winchester finally came into view. He was about a hundred meters away, and appeared to be walking very slowly. Realizing that something was not right, they all ran over to him.

"Mr. Winchester!" Nicola said. "Are you feeling OK?"

"Well, I'm not dead," he replied in a weak voice. "But my joints hurt so bad that I might as well be."

Nicola put her hand on his forehead, and immediately realized that he had a very high fever. "You're burning up!" she said. "We need to get you home to bed."

"Just a slight fever," he replied stubbornly, a bit embarrassed by the worry he was causing them. "I'll be fine once I..."

But before he could finish his sentence, he collapsed onto his knees. A few seconds after that, he toppled over sideways. His eyes were glazed over and his breathing was erratic.

"This is serious guys!" Nicola yelled in a panic. "Brad, call an ambulance! Pete, take off your shirt, run to the river, and soak it in cold water! Neil, go and stand by the corner of the road so the ambulance doesn't miss the turnoff!"

Mr. Winchester was in no state to respond, but he smiled on the inside. Nicola was usually the most timid and shy member of the team, but she had just taken over in a moment of crisis. Maybe they would have a chance against Zoltan after all...

CHAPTER 28

Late that afternoon, Mr. Winchester finally regained consciousness. He was in the ICU at Stoneburg Memorial Hospital. Clearville had no hospital, so the ambulance had to take him to the neighboring city of Stoneburg. Since it wasn't that far away, they rode their bikes there after Mr. Winchester was picked up by the ambulance. After almost eight hours of waiting and worrying, they saw a doctor walking their way.

"Are you family?" Dr. Rollins asked while approaching them. "Are you his grandkids?"

Peter stood up first and shook Dr. Rollins' hand. "Actually, we are his students," he said. "We aren't even sure if he has any family. He's never talked about a wife or brother or kids or anything."

"I see," Dr. Rollins responded. "Well first of all, I must commend you on your prompt action. Calling the ambulance certainly saved his life. But Mr. Winchester is a very, very ill man. I won't go into all of the technical terms right now, but some of his organs are failing. He will need numerous tests done, but he is currently far too weak to run any tests on. So we will have to wait a few days before doing anything."

"Can we see him?" Nicola asked, wiping off some tears with her sleeve.

"You may see him," Dr. Rollins said, "but you won't be able to speak with him. The medicines we are giving him make him very sleepy. He won't be able to carry on any type of conversation. But the good news is that he is currently not in any pain. Anyway, hopefully he will be coherent enough to start talking again within the next week or so."

When they heard the phrase *week or so*, they looked at one another. Everyone was thinking the same thing. For the final five days of their training, they would no longer have a teacher.

Peter felt an additional fear, due to the fact that he still hadn't told Bradley the truth. He was hoping to have Mr. Winchester explain it to Bradley on their final day of training. But now Peter would have to be the one to tell him.

Dr. Rollins took them to the large window in front of the ICU. They could barely make out the old man's face, as he had all sorts of tubes and tape attached to him. After a minute or two in silence, they thanked the doctor and walked towards the front door. Once they were outside, they sat down at one of the picnic tables nearby the entrance.

"This training and stuff has been fun," Neil said. "But, well, seeing him like this… I guess I feel kind of responsible for what happened."

"It's not your fault, Neil," Nicola said. "For all we know, maybe he hasn't been feeling well for days, or even weeks. He just loves training us. He didn't want to let us down."

"More than anything, he wants to see us win," Peter added. Then he paused. He knew this wasn't the best time to explain everything to Bradley. "And since he can't come to watch us, all we can do is go and win this thing, and then march in here with the trophy!"

"You got it Petey," said Bradley, patting Peter on the shoulder. "Let's win it for the old man! Neil, Nik, you in?"

Neil and Nicola looked at each other, and then back at Peter. They both nodded. There seemed to be a silent understanding between them that Bradley didn't need to hear the truth quite yet.

"But who's gonna finish our training?" Nicola asked.

Peter wanted to say something to keep his team confident. "You leave that to me," he assured them. "We'll meet up tomorrow to train. Same time. Same place."

CHAPTER 29

The next morning, Peter outlined what they would do for the final four days. "So here's how it's gonna work," he said. "We are going to create puzzles for each other. You know, tough ones for the other three people to try to solve. But they *must* be solvable, OK?"

Everyone seemed fine with Peter's plan.

"So today we split up and spend the day making our puzzles," he continued. "We'll do mine tomorrow, Nik's on Thursday, and Neil's and Brad's on Friday."

"Cool," Bradley said. "But I can't imagine I'll be able to think of anything that will stump you."

"C'mon Brad," Peter said quickly. "We've been training like crazy for almost two months. Plus you've been watching me do puzzles since I was, like, two years old. I'm sure you can come up with something."

"Well, I'll give it a shot," Bradley said, although

not sounding quite as confident as Peter had hoped.

"Alright guys," Peter said. "Go and get started. You've got all day. And let's up meet at the hospital at six to see how Mr. Winchester is doing."

CHAPTER 30

It was a very long and tiring day for all of them. After splitting up in the morning, no one came up with anything for the first few hours. But somehow, everyone managed to complete their puzzles by midafternoon.

As they had agreed on at the start of the day, they met up outside the hospital front doors shortly before six o'clock.

Peter walked up to the counter while the other three sat in the lobby. "Excuse me," he said softly to one of the nurses. "We are here to see Mr. Winchester. He's in the ICU."

"Just a moment, please," the nurse responded. After looking through some paperwork and typing something into her computer, she looked back up at Peter. "Actually, Mr. Winchester was moved out of the ICU this afternoon. He's now in C-wing, room 202. You can go up to see him, but no more than two at a time in the room. And in all likelihood, he'll be sleeping. If he is awake, he might not be able to respond very well. He's medicated quite heavily."

Peter politely thanked the nurse, collected the rest of his team, and they walked upstairs and down the hallway toward C-wing. Peter and Nicola decided they would go in first. Once they were inside, they could see that Mr. Winchester was not doing well. They didn't know his actual age, but with all the machines hooked up to him, he looked close to eighty. His eyes were closed, so they pulled up the two guests chairs as close as possible to his bed.

Nicola put her hand on Mr. Winchester's forehead. It felt cold and clammy. Peter and Nicola looked at each other, not knowing what to do or say next.

Peter leaned in and put his mouth close to Mr. Winchester's ear. "Mr. Winchester, it's us. I mean, it's Peter and Nicola," he said. "Oh, and Neil and Brad are just outside the door. I don't know if you can hear us or not, but, uh…"

Sensing Peter's nervousness, Nicola tried to help. "We came to tell you that we are not quitting," she said. "You are an awesome leader. You taught us so much."

"He probably can't hear us," Peter said, taking her hand. He was hoping to prevent Nicola from breaking out into tears again. Unfortunately, it didn't work. "Maybe we should just head home and visit him again tomorrow."

Peter should have been focused on the old man, but was selfishly thinking about how he and Nicola were holding hands so naturally. It was almost as if they were a couple. He gently put his arm around her waist as they walked out of the room.

With Nicola crying so hard and Peter thinking about how much longer to keep his arm around her waist, neither one noticed that Mr. Winchester had opened his eyes and was now smiling.

CHAPTER 31

The challenges they had designed for each other were all unique and tough to solve. Peter was extremely pleased by how these final three days went. His team was beaming with confidence. After finishing Bradley's challenge at about 5:00 p.m. on Friday, they started talking about heading to the hospital.

Peter made a suggestion about today's visit. "There's no sense in all of us going to the hospital again," he said. "He's probably still sleeping, and he can't respond to us anyway. Why don't you guys head home, and I'll just go in quickly by myself."

They were all tired and hungry, plus a little nervous about their big day tomorrow. They agreed it was a good plan.

Peter started riding to the hospital. He was really hoping that Mr. Winchester would be awake today, as he needed some last minute advice.

* * *

When he entered the hospital room, he was surprised to see that Mr. Winchester was not only awake, but also sitting up. Peter quickly spotted an envelope on the bedside table with *To Peter* written on the front. Mr. Winchester was still too weak to talk, but was able to point at the envelope and whisper, "open it."

The handwriting looked shaky, leading Peter to guess that Mr. Winchester had written it by himself. Peter read the note to himself silently.

Dear Peter,

Zoltan came to the hospital today. You are to be at the base of Mt. Silverhead at 8:00 a.m. sharp tomorrow. Good luck.

Your friend,

Leonardo

Peter was very familiar with the Mt. Silverhead area. It was one of the most mysterious and intriguing places in the whole country. Like certain places in Egypt, it had once been inhabited by some type of ancient civilization. Zoltan must have chosen this area for their upcoming challenges because he was planning to use some of the old structures or buildings. And since most of the area hadn't been documented yet, it meant Peter had no way of guessing what kinds of puzzles they might encounter there.

Peter put the letter in his back pocket. "We are as ready as we'll ever be," he said.

Mr. Winchester coughed a few times, and tried to clear his throat. Then he somehow managed to quietly say, "I know."

Knowing how weak his teacher was, Peter began to speak without pausing. All the old man needed to do was to listen. "I need your advice, Mr. Winchester," he began. "I have no idea how to tell Brad the truth. If I don't say anything, he'll realize something is wrong when we meet at Mt. Silverhead tomorrow. But if I tell him tonight, you know, explain all about Zoltan and the weather gods and stuff, then he'll call me a liar and quit. I've thought about what to do over and over, but I can't figure out what's best. I have to tell him tonight, but if I do, then he—"

"You lying loser!" a voice said from behind Peter. He turned around to see Bradley standing there. Red with anger, Bradley continued, "I came here to tell you we decided to go for pizza tonight, but instead I learn you've been tricking me the whole time!"

"Brad, wait," Peter begged, hoping to reason with him.

"Shut up!" Bradley yelled, loud enough to be

heard by most of the people in C-wing. "I'm out of here! And you can forget your stupid competition! Or whatever it really is!"

"Please, hold on," Peter begged again. "Just hear me out. It'll make sense if you hear the whole story. Neil and Nik already know everything."

Bradley was now in the hallway. He turned around to face Peter again. "Pete, I told you to shut up!" he yelled. "I don't want to hear another word out of your lying mouth. If I do, then I'll hit you so hard that you'll be staying in this hospital too!"

Bradley stormed away. Peter hung his head in defeat, and turned around to face Mr. Winchester. Peter shook his head, frustrated by how stupid and naive he had been. Not just about the lying, but about thinking that him and his silly team had a chance against Zoltan. And with Bradley out, the chance of success was now definitely zero.

Mr. Winchester picked up a pen and wrote something on the paper on his bedside table. Peter picked it up and read it.

You can do it without Bradley.

Unfortunately, Mr. Winchester didn't really believe what he had just written on the note. He only did it in a desperate attempt to prevent Peter from quitting before tomorrow even arrived.

More than anything, Peter wanted to talk more with his mentor. He needed to hear more words of encouragement. Unfortunately, the old man's eyes were already closed.

Peter headed for the pizza shop. He had to explain to Neil and Nicola what had just gone down at the hospital.

CHAPTER 32

Neil and Nicola listened intently as Peter explained what had just happened in Mr. Winchester's hospital room.

"So Brad's out," Peter said at the end of his long and detailed explanation. "And I don't think we have any hope of doing this without him."

"Well I'm still in," Neil said, "I think we can do it."

"I'm not quitting either," added Nicola.

Peter smiled. At least he wouldn't be on his own tomorrow morning. "But I just wish Brad would have let me tell him the whole story," he said. "He left so quickly. I had no chance to explain. If I had, maybe he wouldn't have quit."

"If he wants out that bad," Neil said, "then I say forget him."

"Don't talk like that!" Nicola responded quickly. "Brad worked just as hard as you did for the last two months." She turned and looked back at Peter.

"Maybe I should talk to him. He might listen to me if—"

"Thanks Nik," Peter said, cutting her off, "but if you knew how stubborn Brad could be, you'd know he's beyond reasoning with. We are a team of three now, like it or not. I wish Brad were with us, but he's not. So we just to have to live with it."

Neil stood up and flexed his biceps. "Tomorrow morning," he said. "We are going show this Zoltan that we can handle anything he can throw at us! No sweat!"

Upon hearing the word *sweat*, Peter looked down at his palms. They were sweating so profusely that the beads were running down his arms and dripping on to his lap. He smiled and looked back up. "Sweat or no sweat," he said, "we'll give him a run for his money."

"You got it!" said Nicola enthusiastically, happy to see Peter looking somewhat positive again. "Now let's all go home so we can get some sleep. We need to be as sharp as ever tomorrow."

They left their money for the pizza on the table, walked out the door, and hopped on their bikes. Even though they'd all be home in time to get plenty of sleep, all three knew that tonight was going to be one of those long nights spent worrying and staring at the bedroom ceiling.

CHAPTER 33

Before going to bed that night, Peter decided to make one final attempt at getting Bradley back on their team. He knew Bradley wouldn't talk to him, so he figured a letter was the only option left. He grabbed a pencil and a blank sheet of paper, and began writing.

Brad,

I know you're angry. If I were you, I would be too. I shouldn't have lied. But I did, and I can't undo that now. Don't blame Neil or Nik. It was my idea, not theirs.

Here's the DVD I got from Mr. Winchester a couple of months back. It's a video of Zoltan demonstrating his powers. Please watch it. I'm sure it'll convince you.

We really need you tomorrow. We won't be able to do this without you. We have to be at the base of Mt. Silverhead by 8:00. That's where Zoltan will have the 8 challenges waiting for us.

Peter

He taped the note to the DVD, and walked quietly towards Bradley's bedroom. He pressed his ear to the door, and could hear Bradley snoring away like a chainsaw. He slid the note and DVD under the gap at the bottom of the door. Now all he could do was hope.

CHAPTER 34

When Peter got out of bed at six thirty the next morning, he felt nowhere near refreshed. He figured he had only slept a total of about two hours. He walked past Bradley's bedroom door on his way to the stairs. He slowed down as he passed the door, wondering if Bradley had noticed the note and DVD yet.

As Peter ate his cornflakes alone at the kitchen table, he found himself suddenly obsessed with the size, shape and contours of his spoon. He started to picture all of the different things a teaspoon could be used for. Once he'd come up with about eleven or twelve, he suddenly realized he had finished his cereal, and there was nothing left in his bowl but milk. He slapped his cheeks a couple of times in an effort to make himself more awake.

He made two peanut butter and jam sandwiches, which had been his favorite lunch for as long as he could remember. Then he grabbed a few juice boxes, some cookies, and a granola bar, and put everything in his backpack. He had no idea how long today was going to be, and wanted to make sure he had something to eat when he became hungry.

Shortly after seven o'clock, while the rest of his family were still in bed, Peter quietly left through the back door and got his bike from the garage. He pushed it to the end of the driveway, trying not to make any noise, and then began riding.

* * *

There was a large sign on the main road indicating the turnoff to the mountain. The narrow road connecting the main road to the mountain was an old dirt one, about two hundred meters long. Peter couldn't see any bicycle tracks in the dirt, which meant he was the first to arrive. He decided to wait near the sign for the rest of his team to get there.

Peter kept looking around while he waited, hoping to catch a glimpse of Zoltan. "I wonder what he looks like..." Peter said to himself, remembering how Zoltan's face was blocked by a hood in the DVD. "Maybe he's got the face of a lizard or something."

Peter giggled at his silly train of thought, which was actually being brought on by his excessive nervousness. In an effort to calm himself down, he sat cross-legged on the ground and closed his eyes. Then he started taking slow and deep breaths.

CHAPTER 35

About fifteen minutes later, Peter spotted Nicola and Neil riding his way. He kept hoping to see Bradley, but knew this was merely wishful thinking.

"Ready to rock, Pete!" Neil said while skidding to a stop to Peter's left. "Let's show this Zoltan guy who the boss is!"

Neil was either unrealistically confident, or was just trying to mask his fear by making ridiculous comments.

When Nicola came to a stop just in front of them, Peter thought she looked different today. There was nothing different about her hair or clothes or anything like that. But her face looked pale and expressionless. Her shoulders hung. She looked terrified.

"Hi," she said while getting off her bike. "I suppose this is where we say something encouraging to each other." After a short pause, she continued, "And then we walk down that path to our doom."

Both Neil and Peter were speechless. Each was waiting for the other to respond first.

Nicola cracked a smile and slapped them both on the back. "You guys are so lame!" she yelled. "I'm just joking!"

After propping their bikes up against some trees, they stood shoulder to shoulder at the start of the path. Peter then began walking first, and Nicola and Neil followed a few steps behind. No one spoke. The only sounds were those coming from the dead leaves being crushed under their shoes as they walked.

After a few minutes of walking, they spotted a single white envelope hanging from the branch of a tree. Peter nervously took the envelope off the branch and slid out the letter that was inside.

CHAPTER 36

With Neil and Nicola looking over his shoulders at the note, he nervously read the message aloud.

> *Follow this path to the entrance. Your challenges lay beyond it. In order to get to them, you'll have to choose the right entrance.*
>
> *You'll see three identical staircases, leading to three identical doors. While one of those is the real entrance, the other two open up to rooms filled with thousands of bees. Your tool is a magnifying glass, and you'll find it hanging from a tree at the end of the path. And you may also use anything that nature has provided.*

"Don't try to figure anything out till we see it

first," Nicola said supportively, taking Peter's hand. "Let's not get ahead of ourselves."

As they continued along the path through the dense forest, Peter found himself daydreaming a little. He kept thinking about the fact that he and Nicola were holding hands again, and couldn't help but wonder if he would ever kiss her. And maybe if he kissed her, she'd become his girlfriend. And if she did, then they could walk around hand in hand at school all day...

But he quickly shot back to reality when they reached the end of the path. As promised, the magnifying glass was there. Neil removed it from the tree and inspected it for a few seconds. Then he handed it to Peter.

"OK, here's how we play this," Peter began. "I take the middle one. Neil, you got the left. Nik, the right. When you get to your door, wait till I tell you what to do. *Do not* touch it unless I tell you to."

Thirty seconds later, they were all standing at the top of their respective steps, staring at the identical light green doors in front of them.

"First," Peter said loudly, "put your ear on the door and listen for any sounds, like buzzing or something."

They all put their ears up against the doors, hoping it would give them a clue about which was the correct one.

"Nothing here," said Neil.

"Nothing here, either," said Nicola. "Quiet as can be."

"Same for me," added Peter.

After pausing a few seconds to gather his thoughts, Peter explained the next course of action. "OK, now kneel down and try to look under the crack at the bottom of the door. Tell me what you can see. One by one. Nik, you go first."

Nicola lay flat on the ground, trying to get in the best possible position to view under the door. "Hard to see," she said. "Looks like a garden or something. Or maybe grass and trees? But the gap is too narrow, I can't really say for sure."

"OK. Neil, you're up," Peter said quickly.

Neil twisted and turned into various awkward positions while trying to look under the door. "Same here," he said. "All I can say is there's lots of green inside."

Peter was already lying on the ground. He also found it next to impossible to get his eye close enough to the ground to see anything. After cursing a few times, he stood up. He realized that Zoltan wasn't going to make any part of this easy.

Peter pulled the magnifying glass from his back pocket. He looked over to Neil and Nicola, who were still awaiting their next instructions.

"Guys!" he yelled. "What do you think we're supposed to use this for?"

"The only thing I've ever used one for was to

burn caterpillars when I went camping," Neil answered.

"Burn caterpillars?" Peter replied, glaring at Neil.

But Neil's comment had given Nicola an idea. "He might be onto something," she said. "I remember, like, a few months ago, watching something on TV about bees. People in this remote village were, like, using smoke to get bees to leave their hives. And then they cut down the hives for the honey. If we could—"

"Set a small fire near each door," Peter said, finishing her sentence for her, "the smoke would bother the bees enough to make them start buzzing around!"

"And then we listen to see which door has no buzzing behind it," Neil added. "And bang! We're in! OK, you guys start piling up dead leaves in front of the doors. And I'll use my *expertise* to get the fires going!"

They quickly put small piles of leaves in front of each door. Then Neil effortlessly used the magnifying glass to focus the sun's rays. He had all three fires going in no time at all. They used their hands to waft the smoke through the narrow gap between the doors and the ground. A couple of minutes later, both Peter and Nicola could hear the angry bees buzzing around like crazy. Neil heard nothing behind his door. Neil gave them the thumbs up, and they ran over to join him.

"You do the honors, Nik," said Peter, gesturing for her to open the door. "It was your idea."

She twisted the knob and slowly pushed the door open. Behind the door lay a small room. It actually seemed more like a garden than a room.

"We're in!" Neil said, holding up his hands to receive high-fives.

Even though he had just told Nicola to lead the way, Peter mindlessly stepped through the doorway first. He was nervous, and didn't realize that he was blocking Neil and Nicola from coming in behind him.

"Make some room for us too, Pete," Nicola said playfully. She put her hands on Peter's waist, and gave him a soft nudge forward.

Once inside, they looked around. The ground was grass, and there were some bushes and a couple of big trees. It was almost as if they were standing in a park surrounded by walls. Neil quickly spotted the next envelope. It was hanging from a branch on the tree closest to the door.

CHAPTER 37

Neil took the envelope off the tree, and read it slowly for everyone to hear.

> *Let me explain what lies ahead. There is a series of 8 challenges. Each one is significantly harder than the previous one. If you can, somehow, manage to solve all 8 before sunset, then you win, and you will replace Mr. Winchester.*
>
> *And I'm sure Leonardo has already pointed this out, but many of these challenges will appear quite intimidating, or even scary. If you would like to quit, simply retrace your steps back to this room. You may then leave through the same door you just entered.*
>
> *But if you do choose to quit, then you*

had better prepare yourself for catastrophic events, unlike anything you've seen even in your worst nightmares.

So let's start! Once you walk past the bushes and trees, you'll come to a long corridor. Halfway down that corridor, there is an envelope containing the instructions for your first challenge.

"You won't see us run out of here like a bunch of babies!" Neil screamed at the sky, as if he thought Zoltan were floating somewhere above them.

"Settle down," Nicola said quickly. "Don't get all worked up. You'll need every ounce of energy you have."

While Nicola was calming Neil down, Peter confidently strode towards the corridor.

"C'mon," Peter shouted back at them. "What are you waiting for?"

CHAPTER 38

They approached the start of the long, narrow corridor. They could see the door at the end of the corridor, and the small table halfway between them and the door. On the table lay the envelope that Zoltan had just mentioned.

"Let me grab that," Neil said, starting to make his way towards to the table.

"Wait!" Peter yelled, grabbing Neil by the shirt. "There could be some kind of trap between here and there. We take it slow and steady, just like we practiced."

They prepared to start the *corridor technique*. This was a cautious method to move safely down any road or path. They had spent a lot of time practicing it during their training. First, they locked arms. This ensured they would be able to help each other immediately should any one of them slip or fall. If Bradley were there, his job would be to walk backwards behind them and make sure nothing surprised them from the back. Today, they would have to periodically check behind them to make up for Bradley's absence.

Nicola was on the left, Peter in the middle, and Neil on the right. Nicola's job was to scan the left wall. Neil would scan the right wall. And Peter would check the floor and ceiling. Before each step, all of them had to say "clear." Although it was very slow, it guaranteed they wouldn't miss any hidden traps.

Four minutes later, they finally reached the table. Thankfully, they hadn't met any surprises on the way.

"Better safe than sorry, right?" said Peter.

Neil picked up the note and read it to Peter and Nicola.

> *For your first challenge, which lies beyond the door at the end of the corridor, your instructions are simple:*
> *1. Enter*
> *2. Close the door tightly behind you*
> *3. Find your way through*

They finished their way to the end, using the *corridor technique* the entire way. The room they were about to enter looked extremely dark. After they walked through and closed the door behind them, they realized it was pitch black.

"Oh, great," said Nicola, her voice a little shaky. "Just what I needed. Zoltan must have spied on us and found out that I'm afraid of the dark."

"Don't worry, Nik," Peter said. "You'll be fine."

"I hope so," Nicola said, searching around in the dark until she managed to find Peter's hand. "But how are we supposed to find the exit?"

"Zoltan has just taken away our best sense, *sight*," he continued. "That means we have to use our remaining four senses. So let's start with *touch*. Put your hands on the door we just came through. Feel around until you can find it."

After a little bit of touching at the air and turning around in circles, all three found the door.

"Neil," Peter said, softly nudging Neil to the left with his elbow. "You are going to move along that wall. Go slowly and carefully. Shuffle your feet along the ground. Keep one hand on the wall, and the other one out in front of you. Nik, you do exactly the same in the opposite direction. And take it slow. There's bound to be traps somewhere."

Neil and Nicola did as told, carefully moving along the wall in opposite directions.

"Pete!" Neil yelled about a minute later. "I just got to the corner of the room. Should I turn around and come back? Or head down along the next wall?"

"Keep going," Peter answered. "But go *slowly!*"

"Roger that," Neil replied.

"Hey Pete, me too," Nicola said. "OK, I'll do the same as Neil."

"Oh man!" Neil suddenly screamed.

"What? What happened?" Peter yelled in reply, wishing he had a flashlight or something to see what was going on.

"I'm fine," Neil said, "but the floor over here just suddenly ends. It's like a cliff or something. I almost fell over it."

"Nik! Stop!" Peter yelled with urgency in his voice.

"OK!" Nicola replied. "Hey, my side's the same. The floor just comes to an end suddenly."

"OK, good job so far," Peter said. "Somewhere over there, there must be a path or bridge or something to get across. Get on your knees, put one hand on the ledge, and then start crawling along it. As soon as you find something, shout."

Peter impatiently waited for one of them to say something.

"Ouch!" Nicola yelled suddenly.

"Ouch back!" Neil said back to her.

"Bad news, Pete," Nicola said. "Neil and I just bumped into each other." If they had just bumped heads, that meant they had met somewhere in the middle. Neither had found a path or bridge.

"Gimme a minute to think," Peter said.

Peter ran through different options in his mind.

"I guess using *touch* on its own isn't going to be good enough," he finally announced. "So let's try *sound*. Lay on your stomachs, with only your heads over the ledge. Then make short, loud noises and listen carefully to the echo."

They got in position, and Neil went first, yelling "Hey!" About two seconds later, it echoed back. Nicola didn't know what word to use, so she just copied Neil. She got the same result.

"All I can say," Neil said, "is that it's a *long* way down."

"Now take all of your change out of your pockets," Peter instructed. "We're going to use it to find the bridge."

The both fished through their pockets and took out whatever change they had.

"Ready!" Neil shouted. "Now what?"

"Drop one," Peter explained, "and then count how long before it lands at the bottom of the pit."

Neil did as instructed. Then he yelled back to Peter, "About four or five seconds!"

"OK, good," said Peter. "Now move carefully along the ledge, in opposite directions. Every meter or so, drop another coin. When you hear it land quickly, stop and tell me."

"Oh I get it," said Nicola. "If it lands quickly, that means it's landed on the bridge, right?"

"Yup," Peter answered.

They both started. On his seventh or eighth

coin, Neil stopped and yelled, "Pete! I think I found it!"

"OK," Peter replied. "Drop one more just to be sure."

Neil did as told. "This is the spot!" he yelled.

"Awesome!" Peter said back. "Nik, slide along until you get to where Neil is. I'm gonna make my way over to you guys."

Peter shuffled along the wall, turned the corner, and made his way to the ledge. Then he kneeled down and crawled along until he bumped into Neil.

"Hopefully the bridge isn't too far down from the ledge," Peter said. "I'm going to hang my arms over and see if I can reach it."

Lying on his stomach, Peter reached down with both arms, but there was nothing there. "I can't reach it," he said.

"Why don't I try?" Neil suggested. "My arms are a lot longer than yours."

"No," Peter replied, a fresh thought popping into his mind. "Neil, you wearing a belt?"

"No. Why?" Neil replied.

"I am," said Nicola, taking off her belt and passing it to Peter.

Peter leaned over the ledge again, dangling the belt in one hand. He heard the clank as the belt buckle made contact with the surface below. He then jerked the belt up and down a few times, listening carefully as he did so.

"There's something down there," Peter said. "And I can't say this for sure, but it sounds like a bridge made of wood. I'll go down first, but you'll have to help lower me. It's a pretty big drop. Once I'm sure it's safe, I'll help you guys down."

Lying on his stomach, Peter hung his legs over the ledge, with Nicola and Neil holding his arms tightly. He slowly slid down further and further, until his toes made contact with the surface below.

Within a minute or so, Peter had helped both Neil and Nicola down as well. He hoped that the hardest part of this challenge was now done.

"This bridge seems pretty narrow," Peter said. "And I can't feel any railings. We crawl across very, very carefully."

After crawling for a few minutes, Peter's head hit the hard rock wall at the end of the bridge.

All three stood up, and put out their hands to feel for the wall.

"No door, though," said Nicola.

"It's probably up above, so we gotta climb up there first," Peter said. "Nik, you're the lightest. Neil and I will boost you up."

They boosted Nicola up first. Then Peter helped Neil up, and finally they helped pull Peter up.

"I'm assuming that the exit side is the same as the entrance side," Peter said. "But we'll still go slowly, just to be sure."

They carefully crawled their way along the ledge until they found the side wall. Then, keeping one hand on the wall, they stood up and shuffled to the corner. Then they turned and shuffled along until they felt the cold metal of the door.

"Voila!" Neil screamed. "We found it!"

Peter felt around until he found the doorknob. He twisted it and pulled open the door. The light which came through was blinding, as they had been in absolute darkness for the last twenty minutes. Shielding their eyes, they walked through the door.

CHAPTER 39

What lay in front of them now looked extremely similar to one of the most traditional and popular amusement park attractions, a *house of mirrors*.

Neil spotted the envelope taped to the entrance of the maze. He opened it quickly and began reading the note inside.

> *I suppose this challenge needs no explanation at all. All you have to do is navigate your way through this maze. Oh, but that would be too easy, wouldn't it? So I'm imposing a time limit. You have 5 minutes, starting now.*

They looked up at the large digital clock on the wall behind them. Just as Zoltan's note had explained, the countdown began. They watched it count. 4:59, 4:58, 4:57...

"I'll go first!" Neil yelled, remembering all of his

childhood visits to the house of mirrors at the local fair. "I'm really good at these!"

"Hold on!" Peter said abruptly, grabbing Neil by the wrist to stop him. "We all go in together, and we stay together. You can't just run ahead. If you get through on your own, how are you going to explain to us how to find you?"

"Oh yeah, you've got a point," Neil responded, looking a little deflated. "But at least let me lead."

"Fine," Peter answered. "You can go first, but remember, no running ahead."

The maze looked no different than any typical one from a county fair. There were lots of windows. There were lots of mirrors. And there were lots of long, twisting paths with tons of corners and dead ends. Neil was leading at a quick pace. Unfortunately, Peter didn't share in Neil's confidence to find the exit so easily. About half a minute after they had started, they were once again standing at the entrance. They had obviously made a wrong turn somewhere. The clock was down to 4:18.

Neil was frustrated, but quickly got ready to start again.

"Slow down!" Peter yelled. "We'll never find our way through like this. We need a way of marking our path as we go, to make sure we don't make the same mistake twice."

"You mean like a trail of breadcrumbs?" Nicola

asked.

Peter took off his backpack and smiled at Nicola. He pulled out the plastic bag with his two sandwiches in it.

"A trail of breadcrumbs," Peter said, "is precisely what I mean."

Neil took the lead again, followed by Nicola, and Peter brought up the rear. Every few steps, Peter ripped off a chuck of bread, and dropped it on the ground. But they quickly ended up at the entrance again. Now the clock was down to 3:52.

Peter wanted to keep his team positive. He knew these mazes were simply a process of elimination. Eventually, they would run out of *wrong* paths, and find their way through.

"Look guys," Peter said. "Now we know which path *not* to take. This time we head down somewhere with no breadcrumbs. Eventually, we'll find it."

At the first fork in the road, where the breadcrumbs showed they had already tried the left, they went right. Peter starting dropping more pieces of bread again, feeling like his plan was working fine. But shortly after, their new path rejoined one that already had breadcrumbs on it. It appeared as if they were caught in some sort of a loop.

They carried on like this for about two minutes. The clock was down to 1:49, but everywhere they went was covered in breadcrumbs. There were no untaken paths remaining.

"Stop for a second," Peter said, a little short of breath and somewhat disorientated. "There must be more than meets the eye to this maze. One of the mirrors or windows can probably be moved. So this time, try to push on every single pane you walk by. Yell as soon as one moves."

They hurriedly began with this plan. Neil was trying all of the panes on the left side, and Nicola the ones on the right. Peter followed behind picking up the bread, to make sure they didn't take the same path more than once. Unfortunately, this didn't provide them with the exit.

"Look at the clock!" Nicola said. "Only fifty-eight seconds left! Now what?!"

Peter heard her, but didn't want to waste any of the remaining seconds replying. He needed to think.

"On your hands and knees!" Peter yelled. "Feel around on the ground for trapdoors! There's gotta be one somewhere!"

They frantically crawled around, but found nothing. The clock was down to 0:24.

"No!" Neil screamed, not wanting to accept defeat. He kicked one of the panels near him, which was obviously made of thick, shatterproof plastic.

Nicola sat on the ground and leaned back

against one of the mirrors. It looked as if she was going to cry.

The countdown continued. 0:19, 0:18, 0:17. Just then, Peter hit on an idea.

"Instead of pushing," he yelled, "try to *slide* them!"

They madly ran everywhere, trying to see if any of the panels would slide. 0:11, 0:10, 0:09.

Miraculously, the one of the mirror panels Neil was testing slid to the right.

"Found it!" Neil screamed. "C'mon! C'mon!"

They bolted through the opening, tripping over each other. 0:04, 0:03, 0:02. They made it out just before the count reached zero.

CHAPTER 40

They were now standing in a three-by-three-meter room with a brick floor. In the center of the room was an enormous pile of keys. The top of the pile was almost up to their knees. And there was another white envelope, which this time was resting on top of the key pile.

While walking up to the keys, they all took notice of the single door on the opposite side of the room. It had a deadbolt on it above the doorknob.

"Uh, guys," said Neil. "It would appear this is a *find the needle in the haystack* game."

"Looks like way," Peter replied. "But let's take a look at the note first."

Peter slid the note out and read it aloud.

> *Keys! Keys! Keys! Don't you just love keys! You may not believe this, but there are exactly 1000 keys here! Only one key can open the lock, but I'm sure you*

have figured out that much already. But what would be the challenge in simply trying key after key after key? You may try only 10 keys. Only 10!

Peter crushed the note in his hand and threw it at the pile.

"Don't get frustrated," Nicola said. "We'll figure it out."

"I've always hated these kinds of games," he responded. "*Find the right one* games. To be honest, I really suck at them."

Neil walked over to check out the lock on the door. It looked like a standard deadbolt that you'd find on the front door of any home. He knelt down to inspect it more closely.

"Well how's this for starters?" he suggested. "Tons of those keys are way too fat to fit in this lock."

"You're right," Peter answered. "So first, let's throw out all of the ones that won't fit."

They began picking up handfuls of keys and sorting through them one by one. They threw all the ones that looked too fat back towards the entrance, and the others they put into a new pile.

This task turned out to be much more tedious than they had thought. It took them close to twenty minutes to finish, and their checks became less and less careful as time went by. When they had finally sorted through every single key, the new pile looked about thirty percent the size of the original one. That meant they had somewhere in the ballpark of three hundred keys remaining. So their odds of guessing were now one in thirty. Not good enough yet.

"So what can we try next?" Neil asked, knowing that they were still nowhere close.

After a few minutes of awkward silence, Peter thought of something to try. "I think I have an idea," he said. "First, we need to find the longest and skinniest key here."

They all began fishing through the pile, holding on to any really long and narrow keys. After a few minutes, they lined up the keys they had selected. There were only nine in total, so it was pretty easy to spot the longest one.

"Game on!" Peter said.

He took the key and slid it into the lock. Then he picked up a second key, and used it to scratch a mark on the shaft of the first key. It marked exactly how far the shaft had gone in. Then he pulled the narrow key out, and showed it to Neil and Nicola.

"Now we know the exact length of key we are looking for," he said. "Let's search for ones with the same shaft length. There can't be that many."

This also took a little longer than he had expected. But once they were done, they were down to around forty or fifty.

"Odds are getting better, eh?" Neil said. "About a one in five chance now!"

Although one in five was way better than the original one in a hundred, it was still too risky. Peter paced around the room, talking quietly to himself.

"I think I have an idea," said Nicola, who had been fairly quiet for the past little while. "Look how some of the keys have one or two really high notches. There's no way that they'll fit in the lock."

They carefully lined up all the keys on the ground, and removed the ones with any high notches. There were only about thirty left now. Since Peter had used up one of their ten attempts when he put the skinny key in the lock to measure the shaft length, they had nine chances left. Their statistical probability of guessing correctly was about thirty percent.

Peter was stumped about what to do next. He decided it was time to test their luck. "This may sound crazy," he said, "but I'm going to give it a try. Maybe I'll have beginner's luck, right?"

Peter randomly picked up one of the keys and took it over to the door, his hand shaking as he slid it in slowly. The key went in smoothly, but it wouldn't twist. He pulled it back out and threw it away.

Neil and Nicola both remained silent. They

weren't sure if Peter was pondering a new idea or not.

Then he picked up another one and tried it. But it was not the right one either.

"Well, the odds were against me anyways," Peter said. "Maybe one of you will be luckier."

Nicola had been counting the remaining keys. There were twenty-seven left.

They sat on the ground and looked at the keys. After a few minutes of pointlessly staring at the small pile, Peter took the initiative again.

"I've tried three already," he said. "So now you both choose three each, and see if you can get lucky."

"Are you sure, Pete?" asked Nicola, shocked by Peter's risky proposition. "Maybe there's something we missed."

After a long pause, Peter replied, "You might be right, but we seem to be out of ideas."

Even though they were just choosing randomly, it took over five minutes for them to pick their keys.

Neil went first. He slid his first key in very nervously. With his eyes closed, he tried to twist it. No luck. The same happened with his other two keys.

Nicola then walked up to the door. She took her first key and rammed it into the keyhole. When it wouldn't twist, she then started jiggling the key around in the lock. Once she had convinced herself that it wouldn't budge, she pulled it out and tried her two other keys. They were also the wrong ones.

Peter gave Nicola a pat on the back, and turned back to the remaining keys on the floor. There were twenty-one left. He had a better chance of guessing someone's birth month than picking the right key.

Peter closed his eyes and put his hand to the ground. He picked up the key his hand landed on. He spun around to face the door, but lost his balance a little, and the key slipped out of his hand. It bounced a couple of times on the stone floor, and landed on the doormat in front of the exit. Peter swore once, and then picked it up and went to stick in the lock.

When Peter's hand was inches from the deadbolt, Neil suddenly jumped in front and blocked the lock with his hand.

"Neil? What are you...?" Peter said. He had no clue what Neil was up to.

But Neil was grinning from ear to ear.

"What are you smiling about?" Peter asked him.

"Step aside, my dear friend," Neil said with a bit of swagger in his voice. "And allow *yours truly* to solve this one."

Peter took a few steps back. Neil bent down, lifted up the doormat, and triumphantly through it off to the side. On the ground, where the mat had just been, lay a single key.

"Dudes!" yelled Neil. "Isn't this where everyone hides their spare key? Now am I the man? Or am I the man?"

Nicola started jumping up and down in excitement.

"Neil, you rock!" Peter yelled. "Now unlock that sucker!"

Neil picked up the key. Without any hesitation, he put it into the lock and twisted it. They all heard the click they had been waiting for. Neil grabbed the doorknob and opened the door.

"Boys and girls!" Neil announced. "Three down! Five to go!"

Peter recalled the part of Zoltan's first note that said the challenges would get progressively more difficult. Although he would never admit it to Neil or Nicola, he was terrified of how hard the *five to go* were going to be.

CHAPTER 41

The room they had just entered seemed like some type of dungeon or cavern. It was large, fairly dark, and the air was cold. And the room was completely empty.

The floor of the room was very unique though. It looked like a giant checkerboard, made of eighty-by-eighty-centimeter stone squares. And every square had a large, yellow *1, 2, 3, 4, 5,* or *6* painted on it. At first glance, it appeared there were no patterns or order to the numbers.

They did a quick count of the floor. It was eight squares wide and fourteen long.

"Where do you think he put the note this time?" Neil asked, hoping to shed some light on how this game was to be played.

While Nicola and Neil looked around for the note, Peter concentrated on the numbers on the floor in front of him. His gut told him that some type of mathematical calculation would show them the right way across.

"Hey, what's this?" Nicola asked. She had just noticed a small box on the ground. It was near the door they had just come through.

"Only one way to find out," said Neil. "Open it up."

Nicola picked up the box and opened it. There were a few small dice inside, but no note.

"Only dice?" asked Neil. "How are we supposed to know what to do with them?"

Nicola took the dice out of the box and looked at them carefully. They were typical six-sided dice, the same as you would use with any board game.

"Mr. Winchester told us this might happen," Peter said with a concerned look on his face. "He said some of the challenges might come with no instructions, and that figuring out what to do would be part of the challenge itself."

"Well dice are only good for one thing, right?" Neil said. "Why don't I roll one and see what happens?"

Neil picked one out randomly, and rolled it gently on the ground beside where he was standing. He had rolled a two.

"Maybe that means I have to walk across by stepping on only the squares with twos on them," Neil said hesitantly. "What do you think? Should I give it a try?"

"Don't see why not," Peter answered. "But go

slowly, just in case you're wrong."

There was a *two* right in front of Neil. He slowly put the toe of his right shoe on the square. He kept the other ninety-nine of his body weight on his back foot. Then he gradually shifted his weight to his front foot. Since everything seemed safe, he lifted his back foot and brought it into the square too.

"This ain't so hard," Neil said. "All I have to do is go from *two* to *two* to *two*, until I get to the other side."

The next *two* was diagonally ahead to the right. Feeling fairly confident now, he bent down and jumped with both feet together to the next square. But the instant his feet lifted from the first stone, it immediately dropped away. It fell into some type of deep pit lying below. Nicola and Peter tried to look down, but it was too dark to see where it had fallen to. Then they all heard a loud crash when the stone smashed into the floor of the pit. Judging from the length of time that had elapsed, Peter figured it was at least three or four meters deep. That was deep enough to cause broken legs, or possibly even something worse, to anyone who fell into it.

Neil gulped. "Well, no turning back, eh?" he said, his face now drained of all confidence.

"Neil, stop there for a sec," Peter instructed. "Nik and I are going to figure out the easiest way for you to get across, and then we'll guide you."

Peter and Nicola carefully looked at the entire board, specifically at the *twos*. They guided Neil, one block at a time, until he was safely across.

"You're up, Nik!" Neil yelled from the other side.

Nicola grabbed a dice and rolled it. It was a four.

Peter took her hand before she had a chance to step on the closest *four*. "Let's plan out your path before you start," he said.

There was only one way to get across on the *fours*. Once Nicola had made it to the other end, she gave Neil a big high-five.

Now it was Peter's turn. He rolled a three. There were a lot of *threes* on the first half of the board, but very few on the second half.

"There's no way across on the *threes*!" he shouted. "Well, unless I can jump 1.6 meters. Which of course I can't!"

"Then why don't you roll again?" Neil suggested.

It seemed like a reasonable idea, so Peter picked up the same dice and rolled it once more. But the instant it hit the ground, every square with a three on it fell at the exact same time. When those squares crashed into the pit below, the boom was unbelievable and the ground shook.

"Uh oh, guess I shouldn't have done that," Peter

said.

He turned away from the checkerboard filled with holes and looked down at the dice. It was a six.

"One way or another," he yelled to Neil and Nicola, "I've gotta get across on the *sixes*!"

He managed to get about halfway across before he found himself stuck. There was a huge gap between him and the nearest *six*.

"You can do it!" Neil yelled. "Just jump there! It's not as far as it looks!"

Peter looked at the big void in front of him. He didn't agree with Neil at all. "No way, Neil," he said, his voice cracking with fear. "I'll end up at the bottom of that pit!"

Peter sighed. He wasn't prepared to make a leap of faith to the next *six*. Unfortunately, he had no other choice. He looked around again. There were no *twos*, no *threes*, no *fours*, and a giant space before the next *six*.

"There's gotta be a better way," he mumbled to himself.

He was panicking now. He couldn't turn back, nor could he go forward. And the dark pit beneath him was the last place he wanted to end up. Peter was close to hyperventilating. He needed to calm down. He sat down and started to take deep breaths.

"What is he doing?" Neil asked Nicola. "Why

doesn't he just try to jump? I mean, like, that's his only choice, right?"

"Because he can't," Nicola replied sharply, her eyes starting fill up with tears.

But Peter was still thinking. He was hoping to find a better solution. "Stupid six!" he yelled at himself. "Why couldn't I have rolled a one, or a five?"

And just as easily as that comment had come out without thinking, the solution came to him too. He stood up and smiled at Neil and Nicola.

"May I ask you," he said loudly, looking very relaxed, "how we get six?

"Huh?" Neil said to Nicola. "He's not making any sense. What's he talking about?"

Before they could even try to answer, he announced, "By adding one and five, that's how! If I put one foot on a *1*, and the other on a *5*, that makes 6! I won't fall!"

"But how do you know?" Nicola said. "What if you're wrong?"

But somehow Peter wasn't worried. He looked around at the nearby *ones* and *fives*, and spotted a place where he knew he could land one foot on each.

Peter looked up in the air. "C'mon math, save me man!" he yelled. Then he bent he knees, and pushed off hard. He simultaneously landed his left foot on a *1* and his right on a *5*. He raised both arms up in celebration. "Yeeeees!"

Neil and Nicola both started cheering.

"You did it! You did it!" she screamed.

Peter finished making his way across. Nicola had another huge hug waiting for him the second he got there. Neil gave him a few hard pats on the back.

Once they felt they had done enough celebrating, they started walking up the stone steps towards the exit.

CHAPTER 42

The exit led to a tunnel, which seemed to be gradually going down. They followed the tunnel deeper and deeper, and eventually it took them to somewhere cold, stinky, and mucky. They were now at the bottom of an old well. It was just like the ones that people in the old days used to get their water from by using buckets and ropes. The brick walls of the well rose up to the ground high above them. Peter guessed they were at least five meters down.

"Anyone good at climbing?" Neil asked, not really expecting to get a response.

Peter touched the walls. They were all covered by a thick layer of slippery moss. Climbing was not going to be an option.

At some point, there had been a ladder mounted inside the well. But all that remained of that ladder now were the holes in the wall where it had originally been attached.

They had been so focused on looking up and around that it took a few minutes before anyone noticed the box and note on the ground. Neil picked up the note and maneuvered it until he had enough light to make out the words on it.

Feel free to use any of these tools to assist you in getting out of this well. You don't want to be stuck down here for too long!

"That's all?" asked Nicola, hoping it had said more.

"Yup, that's it," answered Neil. "Well, let's open up this box and check out what's inside."

They looked inside the metal toolbox. There were screwdrivers, wrenches, a tape measure, a level, some rolls of rope and string, plus various nuts, bolts and screws.

"Well he left us lots of tools," said Neil, "but no wood or anything to build with."

"So there must be something else that we can use them for," said Peter.

They began sifting through the toolbox and pulling out items randomly. Then they would talk about how each one could possibly help them out of their current predicament.

"I think I might be onto something," Neil said. "Lots of the things in here, especially the screwdrivers, are long and skinny. I could slide them into the holes, and use them as hand and footholds to climb up. You know, like a rock climber would."

Neil took out a few of the screwdrivers and started jamming them into holes. They sled in quite easily, and the handles stuck out about four or five inches. Once he had four firmly in, he grabbed the two higher with his hands, pulled himself up, and put his feet on the two lower ones. He then steadied himself, pulled one out, and reached up to put it in a higher hole.

"What do you think?" he asked. "I could just keep working my way up like this."

"But how do you move the ones you're standing on?" Peter asked back. "And if you ever lose your balance, you'll come crashing down."

Neil paused, but decided to try continuing up a little further. Unfortunately, Peter was right. He could get the ones he was holding with his hands in and out easily, but pulling out the ones he was standing on was impossible. He gave up and hopped back down.

Peter grabbed a rope from the box. He knew that leverage could help pull and lift heavy things, even a person's body weight. But he was lost about how to set anything up without someone being up top.

* * *

Twenty minutes later, there were still at square one. They were at the bottom of an empty well, with no feasible way to get out.

"Man!" Peter yelled in frustration. "Is he planning on letting us starve to death down here?"

"Calm down, Pete," Nicola said softly. "Remember what Mr. Winchester taught us? That when you're completely stumped, take a few steps back, and look at it from a different perspective."

There wasn't enough space to take even one full step back, let alone a few. But what Nicola was suggesting certainly wouldn't do any harm. They all leaned back against the wall, hoping a solution would somehow present itself to them on a silver platter.

"Doesn't matter where I look, or how I look at it, a well is a well," Neil said. "Or a hole. Or whatever you wanna call it."

Peter tried to ignore Neil's comment. He wasn't ready to give up yet. He stared straight ahead at the moss-covered bricks.

He held his glare at them, trying not to even blink. Just before his eyes started to water from keeping them open for so long, Peter noticed something he hadn't seen before. On one part of the wall, there was an almost unnoticeable thin line, which had little or no moss on it. The line started on the ground, and went up about a foot and a half.

"What have we here?" Peter asked as he moved closer to touch it.

The closer he got, the more clearly he saw it. There was a very narrow gap in the moss, which was just wide enough that Peter could slide his fingertips in. This was clearly something worth investigating more closely.

"Gimme a hand, Neil," he said. "This has gotta be some kind of door or something. Let's see if we can get it to move by pushing or pulling."

Neil knelt down next to Peter. They both squeezed their fingers into the crack.

"On the count of three, we pull," said Peter. "Ready... One, two, three!"

They both felt something shift. They took their fingers out and looked at the wall again. They could see clearly now that this was not part of the wall, but was actually a tiny door. They pulled and pulled, eventually managing to get it open. Once they had it open a full 90 degrees, Peter lay flat on the ground to look through it.

Peter slid into the fifty-by-fifty-centimeter opening. Then he wriggled through a narrow tunnel, which was at least ten meters long. Once he was finally through and standing on the other side, he yelled for Neil and Nicola to join him.

"I am so glad to be out of that gross well," said Neil once he was through.

"Not as happy as I am!" Nicola added. "Look at

162

me. I'm all covered in slime!"

"C'mon! What's a little slime?" Peter laughed

CHAPTER 43

They spent a few minutes trying to help each other get as much of the slime off as possible. Then they looked around to see where they had just arrived. They were on a fairly narrow ledge, which was about a meter wide. There was a long ladder which led from the ledge down to something below.

They peered over to get a better look at what was down there. It appeared be a large, square swimming pool. As they looked down, they noticed the water in this pool begin to spiral. Within a couple of minutes, the force of the spiraling increased rapidly, and it became an incredibly powerful whirlpool.

Before anyone started down the ladder, they spotted the note taped to the wall. Nicola was the closest to the note, so she grabbed it and read it aloud.

This challenge doesn't require much

explanation, does it? You can see the raging whirlpool below. You can see the ladder that will get you to it. And you can also see the ladder on the opposite side that that will take you to the ledge with the exit. All you have to do is make your way across!

"Better go down and see how big that thing really is," said Neil.

Neil started down the long ladder first. He had only made his way down about five or six rungs when the ladder made a loud creaking sound. He froze, and squeezed his grip on the ladder even tighter.

"Oh, man!" Neil yelled in fear. "The bolts holding this thing to the wall must be all rusted or something. It feels like it could give way at any time!"

Once he was convinced the ladder was sturdy enough to keep going, he cautiously continued his descent. The ladder creaked and moaned with every step. When he was about halfway down, Nicola got ready to start.

"Hold on!" Neil yelled up at her. "It's too weak for more than one at a time! Wait till I'm off, and then start."

Both Peter and Nicola watched nervously. Neil made it to the bottom, looked up, and waved.

Nicola started next. Since she was only about two-thirds of Neil's weight, the ladder remained quiet. But just past the halfway point, she heard a snap. Then she felt the ladder shake a little. One or two of the rusted bolts had just broken off. Even though she knew moving slowly and lightly was important, fear took over. She descended the final few meters as fast as she could.

"Sorry Pete!" she yelled up to him once she was at the bottom. "I panicked!"

Now it was Peter's turn. He was worried about how long the ladder was going to be able to support his weight. As he moved from rung to rung, the ladder made all sorts of noises. It was only a matter of time before another bolt would snap, and Peter desperately wanted to be off the ladder before that happened.

But the snapping noise Peter feared came sooner than expected. He had only come down a couple of meters before a blot snapped, causing a big jolt in the ladder. He stopped, hoping this wasn't the beginning of a chain reaction that was going to bring the whole thing crashing down. Miraculously, the ladder remained fixed to the wall.

A few rungs past the halfway mark, the ladder creaked again, really loudly this time. It wasn't going to hold up for much longer.

Peter looked down. There were still another

seven or eight rungs. It looked like just over a meter and a half to go.

"Jump off, man!" Neil screamed. "Do it now, before it breaks!"

Peter knew he didn't have a choice. He could see Neil and Nicola below him, trying to find the best place to stand to be able to catch him and break his fall. When it looked as if they were both ready, he loosened his grip and let himself fall from the ladder. Neil and Nicola were ready for him, and his landing actually went quite smoothly.

"How nice of you to drop in," Neil said with a smirk on his face.

"Very funny," Peter replied. "Nice catch."

"When you two are finished flirting," Nicola said, "could you take a look at the big whirlpool in front of you, and start thinking about what to do?"

Big was an understatement. The pool was eight by eight meters in size, and the whirlpool in it went right up to the edges. The water was moving with such force that the mist continually splashed up on them, and it was so noisy that they could barely hear each other. There was another small ledge on the opposite side, similar to the one they were currently standing on. And they could see the ladder on the other side which would take them up to the exit. But there were no ledges on the sides. They were going to have to, somehow, go through the vortex of water in front of them.

They could see all sorts of thing floating in the whirlpool. There were buckets, tree limbs, and even some really odd items like tennis balls and toys. The floating junk whizzed around in the whirlpool, progressively getting closer to the center of the spiral. Things were then sucked towards the black center where they disappeared from sight.

"That thing's a death trap," Neil said, swallowing hard. "It's too strong. We'd all get sucked to the bottom and drown."

"No one's gonna drown, Neil," Nicola said, noticing Peter was deep in thought.

Peter remained silent, so Nicola took charge. "Let's start by grabbing whatever we can as it goes by," she said. "Maybe there's something useful in there."

Over the next five minutes, they amassed quite a collection. They had pulled out pails, empty pop bottles, a tire, some shoes, and even a small shovel. They looked at their haul, but nothing seemed to hint at a way to get across a ferocious whirlpool.

Peter got the impression they were waiting for him to suggest something. But instead of giving instructions, he asked for help. "I'm not seeing it," he said. "I mean, like, how can any of this junk help us get across?"

Neil noticed something move near the exit. He grabbed Nicola and Peter, and quickly pointed it out to them. None of them saw what, or who, was just there. But what was left behind was clear. Next to the exit, a digital clock was now hanging on the wall. The timer on the clock was set to five minutes. Before anyone had a chance to comment on how short five minutes was, it began to count down.

"Neil, Pete, look!" Nicola said hurriedly. "Only five minutes! What are we gonna do?"

Peter quickly became flustered. The clock was ticking down, and the pile of junk in front of them contained nothing useful. He started talking to himself. "C'mon, Peter," he said softly. "You can do this. Think man, think. You can't go though it without drowning. And you can't go around it. So that leaves going over it. But how do we get over it?"

Neil and Nicola kept fishing items out of the whirlpool, hoping to find something helpful before the time ran out.

"Over it. Over it," Peter repeated. "But how?"

Peter's concentration was interrupted by a loud jolt. The ladder he had come down about ten minutes ago must have just lost another bolt.

Nicola's eyes instantly lit up. "You've gotta be kidding me!" she yelled. "Guys! Get over here! I think I've got it, but we have to hurry!"

"Really? How?" Peter said.

"Actually, it's easy," she explained. "We rip the

169

ladder off the wall, lay it across, and we will have ourselves a bridge!"

The clock now read 1:55, which meant they really needed to hurry. On the count of three, they all pulled hard, and the ladder broke free from the wall. Then they held the bottom of the ladder, and let the top fall down until it banged down hard onto the opposite ledge. Their bridge was ready.

"One at a time!" Nicola ordered. "It'll never hold all three of us!"

Neil went first, crawling across on his hands and knees. It was much more awkward than expected. When he was finally across, the clock was down to 1:02.

"Neil! Go up the next ladder to the exit! Now!" Peter yelled. "C'mon! Start climbing!"

Neil started up the ladder, but it was also in very poor shape. He knew they would have to climb up cautiously.

Neil got to the top at about the about the same time Nicola had finished her way across the bridge. Then Nicola started climbing up and Peter began on the bridge. But time was running out.

"Only thirty seconds left!" Neil yelled. "Hurry!"

Nicola was about halfway up the ladder. "I'll make it!" she yelled. "But Pete doesn't have enough time!"

The ladder became shakier and noisier. A few bolts had already snapped.

"I'm across!" Peter yelled from below, but he couldn't start his ascent until Nicola was on the ledge.

As soon as Nicola was within reach, Neil grabbed her arm. "Pete! Start now!" he yelled down. "I've got Nik!"

Neil pulled Nicola up on the ledge, and they both looked down to watch Peter's progress.

The ladder was literally falling to pieces. But there wasn't enough time left to climb slowly, so all he could do was race up it and hope for the best.

He was getting close to the top when he heard the noise he was dreading, the loud crack of the remaining bolts giving way. The ladder tore from the wall and started to fall to the ground below.

Peter knew he was a goner. Now it was time to scream.

But out of nowhere, two hands grabbed his arms. The ladder kept falling, but Peter was being held tightly by Neil, who was leaning far over the edge. The only reason Peter didn't pull Neil down with him was that Nicola was using whatever strength she could muster to hold Neil in place.

Neil managed to pull hard enough for Peter to get one hand up to the ledge. Then they heaved with all their might until he was all the way up. Without even bothering to look at the clock again, they dove through the open exit door.

CHAPTER 44

"Nik! That was awesome!" Peter yelled, hugging her tight and lifting her up off the ground.

"No kidding!" said Neil. "How did you figure it out? Me and Pete had no clue what to do."

"I don't know... I..." Nicola replied shyly, cheeks turning a little red.

The victorious trio was now beaming with confidence. They saw the envelope on the floor in front of them, with the words *Final Challenge* printed on it. Peter picked it up and pulled out the note. The message for their final challenge was very, very short.

> *Your final challenge is simple: Find the exit. Find your way out.*

"Find the exit?" Neil asked. "That's it? And I thought the final one was gonna be, like, all complicated or something."

"Not so quick, Neil," Peter replied. "The easier it looks, the harder it probably is."

They looked around the massive room they had just entered. It appeared to be some sort of warehouse, maybe fifty meters wide and at least a hundred meters long. But there was no system of organization in this giant storage room. Some things were stacked and divided neatly on high shelves. Other things were just in massive piles, almost like they had been dumped there from above.

"It'll take too long to search for the exit in here as a group," Peter explained. "Let's split up. We can cover more ground that way."

"Sure," replied Neil. "But who goes which way?"

"Wait," said Nicola. "I don't like this splitting up thing."

"What do you mean?" Peter asked.

"If we split up, and something happens to one of us, no one will be there to help. It's too risky," she said.

"What about you, Neil?" Peter asked. "We all have a say in this."

"I say we split up," Neil replied. "I'll go on my own, and you two go together. We'll cover twice as much ground that way." He paused a few seconds and then continued, "Plus that will give you two lovebirds a chance to kiss while you search, right?"

As soon as Neil finished that remark, Nicola hit

him hard in the shoulder with right hook.

"Ouch!" he screamed in a high-pitched voice. But Neil had learned his lesson.

Peter and Nicola started heading along their wall, and Neil in the opposite way down his. It was only a matter of who would find the exit first.

In less than a minute, Peter and Nicola had reached the corner, so they turned and started walking along the long wall. What stood in front of them was completely impassable though. There was a huge mountain of junk, which looked to be at least five or six meters high.

"Keep both eyes open, Nik," Peter said, taking her hand to help her feel safe. "Although this looks like nothing more than a pile of garbage, there's probably something hidden in it. Some trick or hint or clue or something. We've just gotta spot it."

"OK," Nicola replied, happy to be hand in hand with Peter again. "Maybe something in the pile points to the exit."

"So what we should do," Peter said, "is look for things that are different or out of place."

* * *

Neil had also reached the corner on his side, and had turned to start up the long wall. What lay in front of him was very different from what Peter and Nicola were facing. Along the entire wall was a row of large, identical wooden crates. Each crate was about two meters high, and there was no gap at all between them. When he took a few steps back to get a better look at them, he counted at least fifty.

Neil walked up to one of the crates. He tried to see if he could move it, but it was way too heavy to even budge an inch. And the crates had been nailed shut, so there was no way of opening them.

"What I need to do," Neil said to himself, "is find the clue that tells me which one is hiding the exit."

He walked back about ten meters so he could look at the crates from a distance. They were all identical. And both the ground in front of each crate and the wall behind each one had no special markings.

Stuck for ideas, Neil decided to continue walking past the crates and head for the far wall. That way he could meet up with Peter and Nicola, and get them to come and check out the crates. He was sure that Peter would have some way of figuring out which one the exit was hiding behind.

* * *

Peter and Nicola were slowly walking along the edge of the massive junk pile. They had decided against trying to climb up it, as they didn't want to risk spraining an ankle. They walked in silence, as searching for hidden clues required an incredible amount of focus and concentration. It took a good five minutes to walk past the whole thing.

"Anything?" Nicola asked.

"No," Peter responded, shaking his head in frustration.

"But don't forget this pile could be nothing more than a distraction to throw us off," she said. "The exit could be on Neil's side."

"Maybe you're right," said Peter. "But you know I hate *maybes*. And I'd really hate it if we just walked past the clue without noticing. Let's walk over there and look at it from further away. Maybe we'll spot something we missed.

They walked back a few meters and surveyed the pile again. Nothing seemed to stick out at first. But after taking a few more steps back, Peter thought he spotted something.

"Look towards the left of the pile," said Peter. "Over there, about two meters up from the ground. See where that hockey stick is horizontal? And on both sides of it, see those two wooden beams? Don't you think it looks like a big capital *H*?"

Peter gently twisted Nicola's head so she was facing in the right direction.

"Sure does!" she answered. "And look up there," she said while pointing diagonally up and right of the *H*. "There's an *A*. Well, I think that's an *A*."

They both scanned for more letters, figuring they would eventually be able to spell out a word. They managed to find six letters in total, three *As* and three *Hs*, but couldn't make any sense out of them.

"We've got a bunch of *As* and *Hs*," she said. "But that's it. That doesn't spell anything, does it?"

Peter ran up to the junk pile and kicked a cardboard box as hard as he could. It went flying across the floor. Then without saying a word, he took Nicola's hand. He started walking past the junk pile towards the part of the wall they hadn't checked yet.

While walking, Peter angrily said, "Nik, the letters do spell something. They spell *HA HA HA.* Zoltan's laughing at us! Man that guy is really starting to bug me!"

He looked up at the ceiling and yelled at the top of his lungs, "Ha ha ha! Very funny! You're quite the comedian!"

Realizing Peter was shaking with anger, Nicola squeezed his hand tighter. Then she lightly touched the side of his face with her other hand. When Peter looked down from the ceiling, Nicola's big eyes were focused right on his. For a brief instant, Peter forgot about where he was and what he was doing. He just stared back. His tension quickly drained, and his confidence returned.

"Let's go win this thing," Peter said to Nicola. "We'll continue along the wall till we meet up with Neil. He must have found something over there."

* * *

Neil had made it to the end of the long wall,

and turned at the corner. He knew it wouldn't be long before he'd meet up with Peter and Nicola. The end wall itself was completely bare. As he started along it, he saw Peter and Nicola coming his way.

"Come here!" Neil said excitedly. "I think I know where the exit is! But..." After a short pause, he continued, "But it'll be way easier to show you than to tell you. Follow me!"

They quickly ran over to Neil and let him lead the way. Within a couple of minutes, they were standing in front of the crates.

"So which one is the door behind?" Nicola asked.

Neil sighed, and then turned to face them. "That's the problem," he said. "One of them *must* be hiding the door, but I have no idea which one. I thought maybe you'd have some way of figuring it out."

"Let's do it," Peter responded quickly, anxious to get this final challenge solved as soon as possible. He walked up to one of the crates to see how sturdy it was.

"No dice, Pete," said Neil. "Those things can't be moved or opened."

"We can't open all of them," Peter replied. "But if we can figure out which one is hiding the exit, I'm sure we can find a way to pry it open enough to squeeze through."

"And when exactly did you become so big and strong?" Neil said jokingly, while squeezing Peter's right bicep.

They stood back a fair distance from the crates, hoping they could spot something that Neil had missed. After a few minutes of pacing back and forth, Neil broke the silence. "I'm still not seeing anything," he said. "If there's a clue in there somewhere, then it must be invisible."

Nicola's expression showed that she felt the same as Neil, but Peter appeared to be in his own world. Neil and Nicola were very familiar with this type of silence. They knew it meant Peter's mind was busy contemplating and calculating. Peter looked at the boxes, then at the floor, and then at the wall. After a few minutes of thinking, he turned around suddenly, and looked over at Neil and Nicola. They were familiar with this look too. It meant he had a plan.

"Don't you see?" he said. "The whole time, we've been looking from one vantage point."

"One *what* point?" Neil replied. "What's a vantage point?"

Peter rolled his eyes. He wasn't in the mood for giving a vocabulary lesson. "We've been standing out *here*," he explained, "looking at the crates over *there*. What we need to do is stand on the crates and look out here."

"Huh?" Neil said, still not understanding what

Peter was getting at. "Why?"

"Trust me," Peter said.

The two boys helped boost Nicola up on top of one of the crates. There was no way either of them was going to be able to get up there with her. It was too high, and she wasn't strong enough to help pull them up.

"We can't get up there," Peter said, "so you're gonna have do this on your own."

"I'll try," she replied.

"Just look out. And look down. And look over there," Peter said. "The clue is hiding somewhere. Take your time. Don't worry. You can do it."

She started with a scan of the floor area just in front of the boxes, but it was nothing more than a brick floor. There were a few different colors of bricks, but none formed any shapes, letters, numbers, arrows or anything useful. Next she looked further out, about five or six meters away from where she stood. The ground was still made from the same bricks, but she could see that the position of the bricks was no longer random. She guessed that the bricks had been placed to form symbols or letters on the ground. The expression on Nicola's face made it clear that she had found something.

"I knew it!" Peter exclaimed, giving Neil a high-five.

"One looks like an arrow I think," she said. "No,

wait. Maybe that's not an arrow. No, it's not... Maybe it's a letter. It is! It's an *A*! And hold on, there's another letter over there. An *H*!"

Peter enthusiasm instantly vanished. Those two letters could only mean one thing. Zoltan had left them another *HA HA HA* message on this side too.

"It spells *HA HA HA*, doesn't it?" Peter asked.

Nicola scanned the floor further to her right, and found the other *H*s and *A*s. Peter was right. "Yeah," she replied.

Peter kicked one of the crates, badly stubbing his toe while doing so. Then he swore in pain and hopped away on his good foot. Neil helped Nicola down, and then she explained to him how they'd found the exact same message in the pile of junk on their side.

Neil and Nicola looked in Peter's direction, but neither said a word. Peter wasn't hopping anymore, but he was still limping a little. He definitely shouldn't have kicked that crate so hard. A few minutes later, he walked back to them. The serious expression on his face gave them the impression he was all business.

"We are not going to give up yet," he said. "Back to the drawing board. Back to formula. Back to step one. Whatever you want to say. But we *are* going to find the exit, and soon."

CHAPTER 45

"So what should we do next?" Neil asked, expecting that Peter had already come up with a plan.

"We've looked along all the walls, and there's no door anywhere," Nicola said. "Well, unless it's behind one of the crates. But if it is, we still don't know which one."

"Whoever said an exit has to be on a wall?" Peter said. "We made the assumption that we're looking for a *typical* door on a *typical* wall. Looks like we were wrong. Let's go look everywhere else in here. The exit is hiding somewhere. C'mon! Let's go find it!"

This little pep talk seemed to have worked, as both Nicola and Neil were eager and energetic to get started again. They began walking through the massive room. They navigated their way around the boxes, shelves, and piles of junk. Whenever one of them spotted something promising, they all stopped to check it out. But twenty-five minutes later, after they had covered every square inch of the place, they still hadn't found anything. No exit. Not even a clue as to where the exit might be.

"Man, this is frustrating!" Peter yelled. "What are we missing?"

Neil and Nicola stayed silent. They knew Peter wasn't really asking them, but was just letting off some steam. Peter then began thinking aloud again, mumbling indecipherably in a soft voice. Neil and Nicola both sat cross-legged on the ground and faced away from Peter. They didn't want to cause any distractions.

"How many places can you hide an exit?" Peter asked himself. "I mean, it's either on a wall or on the floor, right? And we checked those, right? And the only place we can't see is behind the crates. But if it were behind a crate, then we surely would have spotted the clue by now, right? So it's gotta be somewhere else then. But where?"

Peter paced around in a small circle, his eyes darting everywhere. He kept mumbling away, getting more and more agitated by the minute.

Then all of the sudden he stopped pacing and put both hands on his head. He looked up and yelled, "How could I have been so stupid!"

He bolted as fast as he could past Neil and Nicola. They quickly stood up and chased after him.

"Don't you guys see?" he yelled back at them while running. "Where's the one place we didn't look? The one place you'd *never* look for an exit?"

"What do you mean?" Nicola replied. She kept running as fast as possible to try to catch up.

After a minute of sprinting, they arrived where Peter had been headed. They had come all the way back to the entrance.

"Uh, Pete," said Neil. "I hate to crash your party, but this is the entrance, buddy. We need to find the exit."

"Think about it," Peter said, still breathing heavily. "The one place you'd never, ever look for an exit is here. Right next to the entrance."

Neil looked at Nicola. They both had no idea where Peter was going with this.

"Come closer, guys," Peter said. "Look."

Neil and Nicola approached the door. Neil spotted it first. About 6 inches to the right of the doorknob, there was a second doorknob, painted perfectly to camouflage it against the brick wall. Neil grabbed the camouflaged handle and tried to twist it, but it was locked.

"I don't get it," Neil said. "There's a door hidden here, but it's locked. What are we supposed to do? Look for the key?"

"No," said Peter, taking Neil's hand off the camouflaged doorknob and putting it on the other one. "That perfectly camouflaged doorknob doesn't open the exit door. It's actually the handle of the entrance. That's why you can't open it. Don't you get it? What we *assumed* was the entrance is really the exit."

Neil and Nicola still weren't following him. "Let me explain," he continued. "Remember when we walked in here at first? The door closed behind us, right? And none of us watched carefully as it closed. Why would we, right? Then we looked around for the note. So we probably moved a little. By that point, the door on the wall behind us, or at least the only one we saw, we naturally figured was the entrance."

"Hold on," said Nicola. "So are you saying that the doorknob in Neil's hand, the one that we thought was the entrance door, is actually for the exit?"

"You got it!" answered Peter, crossing his arms in satisfaction.

"Then open it!" Nicola yelled excitedly. "What are you waiting for?"

Neil twisted the knob. It wasn't locked. They had found the exit.

CHAPTER 46

Of course, they were now standing back on the ledge where they had exited the whirlpool room. Since they had already completed this challenge, they were a little confused about what to do next. But the answer was, literally, written out for them on the ground. Someone had just finished painting *Follow the arrows* in yellow paint. And every meter or so, there was another yellow arrow pointing them in the right direction. They followed the arrows as instructed, which took them along the entire length of the ledge. The final arrow pointed to the wall at the end of the ledge. As they approached the wall, they spotted a hidden door.

"This Zoltan sure likes his camouflaged doors, eh?" Neil said jokingly.

"But at least this one we didn't have to search for," Peter replied.

Peter grabbed the doorknob and twisted it. Then he stood aside, motioning for Nicola and Neil to walk through. He never would have been able to complete these challenges without their help. As they walked through the door towards victory, they were hoping to see a big *Congratulations* sign or something. Or maybe Zoltan was going to be waiting for them in person.

They were finally outside again, at the top of the mountain. A long, windy path lay directly in front of them. They guessed Zoltan was probably waiting for them at the bottom.

Neil raised his arms in the air. "Victory sure does taste sweet!" he yelled.

Peter jokingly slapped him on the back, and then they both turned around to hug Nicola.

"We did it!" Nicola yelled. "We are quite the team, aren't we?"

"This may sound a little cheesy," Peter said, beaming with pride, "but I never doubted our chances for a minute. I knew we'd win!"

Arms around each other's waists, they started down the path. Then they chased, pushed, pinched. and tickled each other, singing and laughing the whole time. They looked like a group of kindergartners playing during recess.

"You know what?" said Nicola. "We must have really tired out that Zoltan guy. He was supposed to make eight challenges for us, right? But I just re-counted in my head, and I'm pretty sure we only did seven."

Peter froze. "Stop walking! Now!" he yelled.

"Stop walking?" asked Neil. "Why? What are you so worried about?"

"I said *stop*!" Peter screamed. He ran in front of them and held out his arms to block them. "This isn't *just a path*. This is the eighth challenge. He was trying to trick us into thinking we'd already won. But, it's not really over yet."

"Gimme a break, Pete," said Neil, pushing past Peter's outstretched arm. "Remember the note? It said that was our last challenge."

"Yes, I remember what it said," Peter said, "*Find the exit. Find your way out.* Don't you see? We found the exit, but that was only the first part. The second part must be getting down the mountain."

"You're paranoid, man!" Neil said, walking backwards down the path. "We won man! We—"

And then Neil suddenly vanished. Of course he didn't really vanish. He had fallen into a large hole.

"Neil!" Peter shouted, running together with Nicola up to where they had last seen him. "Hold on!"

They looked down at Neil, who was lying at the bottom of some sort of pit. As they leaned closer to see how far down he was, they ground gave way, and they both fell in too.

They had just been deceived by one of the oldest

and most primitive tricks in the books, *a hole in the ground, hidden by sticks and leaves*. After a day of amazingly complex and difficult puzzles, they got fooled by something unbelievably simple.

"Anyone hurt?" asked Peter, not being able to see them clearly yet. His eyes were still adjusting to the relative darkness of the pit.

"I'm fine," replied Nicola. "But I think I landed on Neil."

"I'm OK too," said Neil. "And Nik, it's a good thing you're light, or else you would have busted my leg."

"So what did we just fall into?" Neil asked, feeling around for the wall.

"Not sure," replied Peter, as his eyes slowly adjusted enough to see a little. "But I don't plan to be in here for long."

They carefully examined the walls of the pit, looking for anything that would give them a way to climb out. It was way too deep to boost someone out of, and the walls were too smooth and slippery to climb. They were stuck.

"Check by your feet," said Peter. "There must be something in here we can use to help us get out."

Unfortunately, the only things on the ground were the leaves and sticks that had been covering up the hole. It didn't take long for them to realize that this wasn't a puzzle at all. It was simply a trap. A trap with no way out. And it could have been avoided if they had been a little more careful.

Peter sat down. He felt a mixture of disappointment, anger, and confusion. Not only were they going to be defeated by Zoltan, but they were also now stuck in a hole, in the middle of nowhere. And there was no way out.

As time passed, the already dark pit grew even darker. It wouldn't be long before it would be pitch black. Peter kept reminding himself about the rules, which were that they had to complete the final challenge before sunset. If they didn't, then Zoltan would win, and the destruction which he had promised would start again.

Peter felt a hand pat him on the back. "I screwed up, man," said Neil. "I blew it for all of us. Now we are stuck down here. Man, I was so stupid!"

Peter didn't know how to reply. He still couldn't believe that Neil had ignored his warning and ran ahead.

Not knowing what to say to each other, they all sat down. Then suddenly, their depressing silence was broken. They heard the rustling of leaves up above. Someone, or something, was coming their way.

"Help us!" screamed Nicola. "Down here! Help! Help!"

They all looked up, but since it was so close to sunset, they couldn't see much. Then a very bright light, from some type of flashlight, was shone into their eyes.

Nicola waved her arms frantically and yelled, "Help us! Please! We're stuck!"

Whoever was holding the flashlight had no intention of speaking. Instead, he or she dropped the flashlight into the hole. It landed near Neil's foot. He quickly picked it up, and aimed it upward to see who their rescuer was.

But all they saw was a hand, which was holding something small. The hand then let go of whatever it was holding, and it began fluttering down slowly. As it got closer to them, they realized it was an envelope. After it landed, Neil aimed the flashlight directly at it. It was a small envelope, just like the ones they had received all of their puzzle instructions in. Peter took the note out, and softly read its contents.

So close. You did quite well. 7 out of 8. But close is not good enough.

Anyway, now 3 of you are trapped in this pit, and the fourth will soon become lost in the darkness. So unless you can miraculously pull a rabbit out of a hat, (or should say out of a hole - ha ha ha) then I suppose you lose!

Peter crushed the note into a ball, and threw it on the ground. Not only had they lost, but now their faces were being rubbed in it.

"What does he mean by the *fourth* person?" Nicola asked a couple minutes later.

"He must mean Brad," Peter replied expressionlessly. "I guess Zoltan has no idea that Bradley quit on us before we even came today."

But all of the sudden, Peter's face changed. "Hold on a second," he said. "If Zoltan just watched three out of four people fall into this hole, then that means someone else must be up there. And they must be close by. We know it's not Brad. It must be a hiker or camper or something. Anyway, I don't care who it is. If someone is up there, they can help us get out!"

All three of them began screaming for help as loud as they could. Neil aimed the flashlight up, hoping to make their location easier to spot. After a few minutes of yelling, they paused to catch their breath. Then they heard footsteps coming quickly their way.

A face appeared over the ledge. "Figured you couldn't win this thing without me!" said Bradley, dropping a rope ladder down to them. "Hurry up and climb! Zoltan hasn't won yet!"

"Brad?!" Peter exclaimed in utter disbelief. "How did—"

"Mr. Winchester came to see me today," Bradley

yelled down, cutting Peter off. "Anyway, there's no time to talk now! C'mon, climb! We can still win this if we hurry!"

One at a time, they frantically climbed up the rope ladder. Sunset was very, very close. When all three were out, Bradley quickly passed everyone headlamps, which he had already turned on. These headlamps would make it easy to see the path out in the darkening forest.

"Never come unprepared!" Bradley said while pointing at his huge backpack. "OK, let's go! Run in single file! Follow my steps exactly! We don't want you falling in any more holes!"

Bradley led them down the path. He had dropped bright yellow markers on all of the other hidden pits he had passed on his way up. As long as they stayed away from those markers, they'd be able to make it down safely. Peter could see quite a few markers ahead of them, meaning they would have had no chance at all without Bradley's help.

Peter needed an explanation for Bradley's timely arrival. "What do you mean he came to see you?" he asked Bradley as they weaved their way between the traps. "How did he get out of the hospital?"

"No clue," Bradley replied. "He just showed up at our house at about lunchtime. He made me watch that DVD, and then he begged me to come out here."

"But we'd already started," Peter said back quickly. "Why would—"

"Not to join you," Bradley said, cutting Peter off again. "He said he was convinced that Zoltan would pull some trick to prevent you from winning. He wanted me to come out here and watch for anything suspicious."

"You mean he thought Zoltan was gonna cheat?" Peter asked.

"Something like that," Bradley replied. "Anyway, so I put all our outdoor gear in a backpack and rode out here. And after walking around the mountain for an hour or so, I spotted some guy in a hood setting up traps."

"A hooded guy?" Peter asked as they ran past the last of the traps. "You mean Zoltan?"

"I guess," Bradley replied. "So I hid in the bushes, and watched where he set the traps. Once he got far enough away, I marked the ones I remembered. And then I just hid and waited for any sign of you guys."

"And when you heard us screaming," Nicola said loudly from behind Peter, "you ran over to help!"

"To help?" Bradley said back, giggling a little. "You mean to *save* you! But how did you manage to fall in the only hole I missed? I mean, like, what are the odds of that?"

"Look!" Neil yelled. "There's the exit!"

The exit was less than fifty meters away now. It was actually nothing more than a gate at the end of the path. They all sprinted, using whatever energy they had left. They needed to get through that gate before it was too late.

They burst through the gate and collapsed on the ground in exhaustion. A tiny sliver of the sun was still visible on the horizon. They had made it in time.

Peter stood up first. He aimed his headlamp towards the road. A short distance away, two people were standing and looking their way. One was Mr. Winchester. How he had managed to get out of his hospital bed was a mystery of its own. And the other was Zoltan. Neither of them moved, so Peter took it as a hint that they were expecting him to walk over.

He approached them quickly. He really wanted to see the face of this supernatural being close up. But Zoltan's face was once again hidden by a large hood. Just before Peter got to them, Zoltan shook Mr. Winchester's hand. Then without saying a word, Zoltan turned and walked away.

"Well done, Peter," Mr. Winchester said in a raspy voice. "I am so pleased, and honored, to have you take over for me. You're perfectly capable of keeping Zoltan entertained. People will be safe again, thanks to you."

He handed Peter a small box. Peter opened it

and looked at the two things inside. One was a key, and the other was a piece of paper with an address written on it.

"There's a shed at that address," Mr. Winchester said. "And you can open it with the key. Inside the shed, you'll find everything I've ever used while creating puzzles for Zoltan. Notes, sketches, tools, everything. That's where I came up with, created, and stored all of my puzzles. Use anything you can. I'm sure it will help."

Mr. Winchester appeared to have tears forming in his eyes. He turned and started limping slowly away. To where? Peter had no idea.

CHAPTER 47

Peter looked up the clock on the far side of the classroom. He still had sixteen minutes left of listening to Mr. Pendleton's boring geographical explanations. Then he shot a glance over to Nicola. She winked at Peter again, for the twelfth time that class.

"And this may be straying from the textbook a bit," his teacher said. "But haven't you all noticed those nasty storms seemed to have become a thing of the past?"

No one was sure if that question was being asked to the class, or if Mr. Pendleton was just rambling away and killing time until the bell.

"I spoke with a friend at the weather bureau," he continued. "And he informed me the storms have stopped all over the globe."

Peter counted Nicola's thirteenth wink. He couldn't wait to get out of school today. They were now officially a couple, despite all of her friends' objections. And since today was Friday, they were going to the movies after school. They would watch a mystery again, hoping something in the movie would provide them with some inspiration or ideas to use on their next puzzle for Zoltan.

Then tomorrow, Peter and Nicola would spend the day at the secret little hideaway holding all of Mr. Winchester's supplies. They went there every Saturday, often staying until it was time to head home for dinner. They used Saturday as their day to prepare Zoltan's weekly puzzle. And if they could get it ready quickly tomorrow, Peter knew they'd spend the rest of the afternoon telling stories and hanging out. He wondered if tomorrow would be the day he'd finally get enough courage to try to give Nicola a kiss.

Neil kicked Peter's chair. "Sleeping again, Pete?" he asked. "Or just daydreaming about your girlfriend?"

Peter looked up. Other than Neil, he was the only one left in the room. Nicola was standing at the door with her arms crossed.

"Oops," Peter said. "Must have dozed off."

He ran to the door and put his arm around Nicola's waist. They started walking together to their final class of the day, math. Unfortunately, they still had sixty minutes, or three thousand and six hundred seconds, of school left before they could head to the theater.

"I've got an awesome idea for the next puzzle," she said as they walked upstairs. "Wanna hear?"

"I certainly do," he replied. "But not here. If people hear you talking about that kind of stuff, they'll think you're as weird as me!"

Nicola giggled. The bell had already rung, so they were going to be late for class. But on a good note, they only had 3555 seconds of math left to go.

Thank you for reading *Puzzled*. I hope you liked it! If you enjoyed this book, then I'd like to ask you for a favor: would you be kind enough to leave a review for this book on Amazon? It would be enormously helpful for me. Thank you so much!

And if you have any comments or questions, please e-mail me anytime (p.j.nichols.puzzled@gmail.com). I'm currently working on the sequel, and I would appreciate any suggestions about what you'd like to see in the next part of Peter's adventure!

Sincerely,
P.J. Nichols

Acknowledgements

My mom, who answered every single "What if...?" question I asked while growing up. Her answers were all correct. *The sky didn't fall* and the *the sun didn't suddenly disappear.* Well, at least not yet, but... "What if they do?"

My dad, who is living proof that you don't have to be tall, strong, or get straight As at school to become a superstar. More than anything, he showed me how fun it was to make people happy. Everything I now try to do for my son I learned from him, especially the storytelling.

My three brothers: a "genius," a "creative mastermind," and an "athlete," who made growing up a true adventure, filled with countless fun memories.

My wife, who loves and supports me in everything I do, despite all of my quirks.

My son, whose curiosity in taking on new challenges inspired me to write this book.

Thank you to everyone who helped me along on my book writing journey. You are all awesome. I couldn't have done it without you.

About the Author

P.J. Nichols loves games. But not the kind you buy at stores. And not the kind you practice and practice and practice to get good at. He likes the games you think up and make by yourself.

No matter where he is, or what things are around him, P.J. will find a way to create a game. One where you race. Or one where you build. Or one where you think. Or maybe even one where you do all three.

Back when he was growing up with his three brothers in Canada, he was constantly making games. Neighborhood kids (and even some of their parents) would run over to join in. There was never a boring moment in or around the Nichols' house.

P.J. is sure that his debut novel, Puzzled, will have you rushing to think up games for your friends, brothers, sisters, or parents to try!